All Creatures Great and Small

Ruskin Bond is known for his signature simplistic and witty writing style. He is the author of several bestselling short stories, novellas, collections, essays and children's books; and has contributed a number of poems and articles to various magazines and anthologies. At the age of twenty-three, he won the prestigious John Llewellyn Rhys Prize for his first novel, *The Room on the Roof*. He was also the recipient of the Padma Shri in 1999, Lifetime Achievement Award by the Delhi government in 2012 and the Padma Bhushan in 2014.

Born in 1934, Ruskin Bond grew up in Jamnagar, Shimla, New Delhi and Dehradun. Apart from three years in the UK, he has spent all his life in India, and now lives in Landour, Mussoorie, with his adopted family.

RUSKIN BOND

All Creatures Great and Small

RUPA

Published by
Rupa Publications India Pvt. Ltd 2022
7/16, Ansari Road, Daryaganj
New Delhi 110002

Sales centres:
Allahabad Bengaluru Chennai
Hyderabad Jaipur Kathmandu
Kolkata Mumbai

ISBN: 978-93-5520-344-1

First impression 2022

10 9 8 7 6 5 4 3 2 1

CONTENTS

INTRODUCTION

How many of us have spent hours looking at animal videos on the Internet? Or have spent countless hours following the shenanigans of cats, dogs, goats and/or elephants? On a stressful day, or even a non-eventful day, these videos intrigue us and make us smile. Many pet owners look forward to the moment when they step into the house and their pets greet them with affectionate enthusiasm. You can sit for hours and have conversations with your pets.

Humans often try to understand the ways of the animal kingdom. Hours and hours are spent in forests making documentaries or in labs studying animals. We've always been fascinated by them, even mystified. One glimpse of a majestic tiger or the roar of a lion, the gallop of a horse or slither of a python; we watch in wonder as animals go about their day around us.

This book is a collection of stories that expands on and records this peculiar relationship between humans and animals. It is a book of intrigue, adventure, joy and loyalty. Starting with the warring relationship of a monkey and a python, to the story of a determined snail, to the adventures of an owl.

This collection of stories and personal essays is for children and adults alike—the only prerequisite to read this book is love for and curiosity about the creatures we find in nature!

Ruskin Bond

ALL CREATURES GREAT AND SMALL

Instead of having brothers and sisters to grow up with in India, I had as my companions an odd assortment of pets, which included a monkey, a tortoise, a python and a Great Indian Hornbill. The person responsible for all this wildlife in the home was my grandfather. As the house was his own, other members of the family could not prevent him from keeping a large variety of pets, though they could certainly voice their objections; and as most of the household consisted of women—my grandmother, visiting aunts and occasional in-laws (my parents were in Burma at the time)—Grandfather and I had to be alert and resourceful in dealing with them. We saw eye to eye on the subject of pets, and whenever Grandmother decided it was time to get rid of a tame white rat or a squirrel, I would conceal them in a hole in the jackfruit tree; but unlike my aunts, she was generally tolerant of Grandfather's hobby, and even took a liking to some of our pets.

Grandfather's house and menagerie were in Dehra and I remember travelling there in a horse-drawn buggy. There were cars in those days—it was just over twenty years ago—but in the foothills a tonga was just as good, almost as fast and certainly more dependable when it came to getting across the swift little Tons river.

During the rains, when the river flowed strong and deep, it was impossible to get across except on a hand-operated ropeway; but in the dry months, the horse went splashing through, the carriage wheels churning through clear mountain water. If the horse found the going difficult, we removed our shoes, rolled up our skirts or trousers and waded across.

When Grandfather first went to stay in Dehra, early in the century, the only way of getting there was by the night mail coach. Mail ponies, he told me, were difficult animals, always attempting to turn around and get into the coach with the passengers. It was only when the coachman used his whip liberally, and reviled the ponies' ancestors as far back as their third and fourth generations, that the beasts could he persuaded to move. And once they started, there was no stopping them. It was a gallop all the way to the first stage, where the ponies were changed to the accompaniment of a bugle blown by the coachman.

At one stage of the journey, drums were beaten; and if it was night, torches were lit to keep away the wild elephants who, resenting the approach of this clumsy caravan, would sometimes trumpet a challenge and throw the ponies into confusion.

◆

Grandfather disliked dressing up and going out, and was only too glad to send everyone shopping or to the pictures—Harold Lloyd and Eddie Cantor were the favourites at Dehra's small cinema—so that he could be left alone to feed his pets and potter about in the garden. There were a lot of animals to be fed, including, for a time, a pair of Great Danes who had such enormous appetites that we were forced to give them away to a more affluent family.

The Great Danes were gentle creatures, and I would sit astride one of them and go for rides round the garden. Inspite of their size, they were very sure-footed and never knocked over people or chairs. A little monkey, like Toto, did much more damage.

Grandfather bought Toto from a tonga-owner for the sum of five rupees. The tonga-man used to keep the little, red monkey tied to a feed-trough, and Toto looked so out of place there—almost conscious of his own incongruity—that Grandfather immediately decided to add him to our menagerie.

Toto was really a pretty, little monkey. His bright eyes sparkled with mischief beneath deep-set eyebrows, and his teeth, a pearly-white, were often on display in a smile that frightened the life out of elderly Ango-Indian ladies. His hands were not those of a Tallulah Bankhead (Grandfather's only favourite actress), but were shrivelled and dried-up, as though they had been pickled in the sun for many years. But his fingers were quick and restless; and his tail, while adding to his good looks—Grandfather maintained that a tail would add to anyone's good looks—often performed the service of a third hand. He could use it to hang from a branch; and it was capable of scooping up any delicacy that might be out of reach of his hands.

Grandmother, anticipating an outcry from other relatives, always raised objections when Grandfather brought home some new bird or animal; and so for a while we managed to keep Toto's presence a secret by lodging him in a little closet opening into my bedroom wall. But in a few hours he managed to dispose of Grandmother's ornamental wallpaper and the better part of my school blazer. He was transferred to the stables for a day or two, and then Grandfather had to make a trip to neighbouring Saharanpur to collect his railway pension. Anxious to keep Toto out of trouble, he decided to take the monkey along with him.

Unfortunately I could not accompany Grandfather on this trip, but he told me about it afterwards.

A black kit-bag was provided for Toto. When the strings of the bag were tied, there was no means of escape from within, and the canvas was too strong for Toto to bite his way through. His initial efforts to get out only had the effect of making the bag roll about on the floor, or occasionally jump in the air—an exhibition that attracted a curious crowd of onlookers on the Dehra railway platform.

Toto remained in the bag as far as Saharanpur, but while Grandfather was producing his ticket at the railway turnstile, Toto managed to get his hands through the aperture where the bag was tied, loosened the strings, and suddenly thrust his head through the opening.

The poor ticket-collector was visibly alarmed; but with great presence of mind, and much to the annoyance of Grandfather, he said, 'Sir, you have a dog with you. You'll have to pay for it accordingly.'

In vain did Grandfather take Toto out of the bag to prove that a monkey was not a dog or even a quadruped. The ticket-collector, now thoroughly annoyed, insisted on classing Toto as a dog; and three rupees and four annas had to be handed over as his fare. Then Grandfather, out of sheer spite, took out from his pocket a live tortoise that he happened to have with him, and said, 'What must I pay for this, since you charge for all animals?'

The ticket-collector retreated a pace or two; then advancing again with caution, he subjected the tortoise to a grave and knowledgeable stare.

'No ticket is necessary, sir,' he finally declared. 'There is no charge for insects.'

When we discovered that Toto's favourite pastime was catching mice, we were able to persuade Grandmother to let us keep him. The unsuspecting mice would emerge from their holes at night to pick up any corn left over by our pony; and to get at it they had to run the gauntlet of Toto's section of the stable. He knew this, and would pretend to be asleep, keeping, however, one eye open. A mouse would make a rush—in vain; Toto, as swift as a cat, would have his paws upon him... Grandmother decided to put his talents to constructive use by tying him up one night in the larder, where a guerrilla-hand of mice were playing havoc with our food supplies.

Toto was removed from his comfortable bed of straw in the stable, and chained up in the larder, beneath shelves of jam-pots and other delicacies. The night was a long and miserable one for Toto, who must have wondered what he had done to deserve such treatment. The mice scampered about the place, while he, most uncatlike, lay curled up in a soup tureen, trying to snatch some sleep. At dawn, the mice returned to their holes; Toto awoke, scratched himself, emerged from the soup tureen and looked about for something to eat. The jam-pots attracted his notice, and it did not take him long to prise open the covers. Grandmother's treasured jams—she had made most of them herself—disappeared in an amazingly short time. I was present when she opened the door to see how many mice Toto had caught. Even the rain god Indra could not have looked more terrible when planning a thunderstorm; and the imprecations Grandmother hurled at Toto were surprising coming from someone who had been brought up in the genteel Victorian manner.

The monkey was later reinstated in Grandmother's favour. A great treat for him on cold winter evenings was the large bowl of warm water provided by Grandmother for his bath. He would bathe himself, first of all gingerly testing the temperature of the water with his fingers. Leisurely he would step into the bath, first one foot, then the other, as he had seen me doing, until he was completely sitting down in it. Once comfortable, he would take the soap in his hands or feet, and rub himself all over. When he found the water becoming cold, he would get out and run as quickly as he could to the fire, where his coat soon dried. If anyone laughed at him during this performance, he would look extremely hurt, and refuse to go on with his ablutions.

One day, Toto nearly succeeded in boiling himself to death.

The large kitchen kettle had been left on the fire to boil for tea; and Toto, finding himself for a few minutes alone with it, decided to take the lid off. On discovering that the water inside was warm, he got into the kettle with the intention of having a bath, and sat down with his head protruding from the opening. This was very pleasant for some time, until the water began to simmer. Toto raised himself a little, but finding it cold outside, sat down again. He continued standing and sitting for some time, not having the courage to face the cold air. Had it not been for the timely arrival of Grandmother, he would have been cooked alive.

If there is a part of the brain especially devoted to mischief, that part must have been largely developed in Toto. He was always tearing things to bits, and whenever one of my aunts came near him, he made every effort to get hold of her dress and tear a hole in it. A variety of aunts frequently came to stay with my grandparents, but during Toto's stay they limited their visits to a day or two, much to Grandfather's relief and Grandmother's annoyance.

Toto, however, took a liking to Grandmother, inspite of the beatings he often received from her. Whenever she allowed him the liberty, he would lie quietly in her lap instead of scrambling all over her as he did on most people.

Toto lived with us over a year, but the following winter, after too much bathing, he caught pneumonia. Grandmother wrapped him in flannel, and Grandfather gave him a diet of chicken soup and Irish stew; but Toto did not recover. He was buried in the garden, under his favourite mango tree.

◆

Perhaps it was just as well that Toto was no longer with us when Grandfather brought home the python, or his demise might have been less conventional. Small monkeys are a favourite delicacy with pythons.

Grandmother was tolerant of most birds and animals, but she drew the line at reptiles. She said they made her blood run cold. Even a handsome, sweet-tempered chameleon had to be given up. Grandfather should have known that there was little chance of his being allowed to keep the python. It was about four feet long, a young one, when Grandfather bought it from a snake-charmer for six rupees, impressing the bazaar crowd by slinging it across his shoulders and walking home with it. Grandmother nearly fainted at the sight of the python curled round Grandfather's throat.

'You'll be strangled!' she cried. 'Get rid of it at once!'

'Nonesense,' said Grandfather. 'He's only a young fellow.

He'll soon get used to us.'

'Will he, indeed?' said Grandmother. 'But I have no intention of getting used to him. You know quite well that your cousin Mabel is coming to stay with us tomorrow. She'll leave us the minute she knows there's a snake in the house.'

'Well, perhaps we ought to show it to her as soon as she arrives,' said Grandfather, who did not look forward to fussy Aunt Mabel's visits any more than I did.

'You'll do no such thing,' said Grandmother.

'Well, I can't let it loose in the garden,' said Grandfather with an innocent expression. 'It might find its way into the poultry house, and then where would we be?'

'How exasperating you are!' grumbled Grandmother. 'Lock the creature in the bathroom, go back to the bazaar, find the man you bought it from and get him to come and take it back.'

In my awestruck presence, Grandfather had to take the python into the bathroom, where he placed it in a steep-sided tin tub. Then he hurried off to the bazaar to look for the snake-charmer, while Grandmother paced anxiously up and down the verandah. When he returned looking crestfallen, we knew he hadn't been able to find the man.

'You had better take it away yourself,' said Grandmother, in a relentless mood. 'Leave it in the jungle across the river-bed.'

'All right, but let me give it a feed first,' said Grandfather; and producing a plucked chicken, he took it into the bathroom, followed, in single file, by me, Grandmother and a curious cook and gardener.

Grandfather threw open the door and stepped into the bathroom. I peeped round his legs, while the others remained well behind. We couldn't see the python anywhere.

'He's gone,' announced Grandfather. 'He must have felt hungry.'

'I hope he isn't too hungry,' I said.

'We left the window open,' said Grandfather, looking embarrassed.

A careful search was made of the house, the kitchen, the garden, the stable and the poultry shed; but the python couldn't be found anywhere.

'He'll be well away by now,' said Grandfather reassuringly.

'I certainly hope so,' said Grandmother, who was half way between anxiety and relief.

Aunt Mabel arrived next day for a three-week visit, and for a couple of clays Grandfather and I were a little apprehensive in case the python made a sudden reappearance; but on the third day, when he didn't show up, we felt confident that he had gone for good.

And then, towards evening, we were startled by a scream from the garden. Seconds later, Aunt Mabel came flying up the verandah steps, looking as though she had seen a ghost.

'In the guava tree!' she gasped. 'I was reaching for a guava, when I saw it staring at me. The *look* in its eyes! As though it would *devour* me—'

'Calm down, my dear,' urged Grandmother, sprinkling her with eau-de-cologne. 'Calm down and tell us what you saw.'

'A snake!' sobbed Aunt Mabel. 'A great boa-constrictor. It must have been twenty feet long! In the guava tree. Its eyes were terrible. It looked at me in such a *queer* way....'

My grandparents looked significantly at each other, and Grandfather said, 'I'll go out and kill it,' and sheepishly taking hold of an umbrella, sallied out into the garden. But when he reached the guava tree, the python had disappeared.

'Aunt Mabel must have frightened it away,' I said.

'Hush,' said Grandfather. 'We mustn't speak of your aunt in that way.' But his eyes were alive with laughter.

After this incident, the python began to make a series of appearances, often in the most unexpected places. Aunt Mabel had another fit of hysterics when she saw him admiring her from under a cushion. She packed her bags, and Grandmother made us intensify the hunt.

Next morning, I saw the python curled up on the dressing-table, gazing at his reflection in the mirror. I went for Grandfather, but by the time we returned the python had moved elsewhere. A little later he was seen in the garden again. Then he was back on the dressing-table, admiring himself in the mirror. Evidently, he had become enamoured with his own reflection. Grandfather observed that perhaps the attention he was receiving from everyone had made him a little conceited.

'He's trying to look better for Aunt Mabel,' I said; a remark that I instantly regretted, because Grandmother overheard it, and brought the flat of her broad hand down on my head.

'Well, now we know his weakness,' said Grandfather.

'Are you trying to be funny too?' demanded Grandmother, looking her most threatening.

'I only meant he was becoming very vain,' said Grandfather hastily. 'It should be easier to catch him now.'

He set about preparing a large cage with a mirror at one end. In the cage he left a juicy chicken and various other delicacies, and fitted up the opening with a trap-door. Aunt Mabel had already left by the time we had this trap ready, but we had to go on with the project because we couldn't have the python prowling about the house indefinitely.

For a few days nothing happened, and then, as I was leaving for school one morning, I saw the python curled up in the cage. He had eaten everything left out for him, and was relaxing in front of the mirror with something resembling a smile on his face—if you can imagine a python smiling... I lowered the trap-door gently, but the python took no notice; he was in raptures over his handsome reflection. Grandfather and the gardener put the cage in the ponytrap, and made a journey to the other side of the river-bed. They left the cage in the jungle, with the trap-door open.

'He made no attempt to get out,' said Grandfather later. 'And I didn't have the heart to take the mirror away. It's the first time I've seen a snake fall in love.'

◆

'And the frogs have sung their old song in the mud...' This was Grandfather's favourite quotation from Virgil, and he used it whenever we visited the rain-water pond behind the house where there were quantities of mud and frogs and the occasional water buffalo. Grandfather had once brought a number of frogs into the house. He had put them in a glass jar, left them on a window-sill, and then forgotten all about them. At about four o' clock in the morning, the entire household was awakened by a loud and fearful noise, and Grandmother and several nervous relatives gathered in their nightclothes on the verandah. Their timidity changed to fury when they discovered that the ghastly sounds had come from Grandfather's frogs. Seeing the dawn breaking, the frogs had with one accord begun their morning song.

Grandmother wanted to throw the frogs, bottle and all, out of the window; but Grandfather said that if he gave the bottle a good shaking, the frogs would remain quiet. He was obliged to keep awake, in order to shake the bottle whenever the frogs showed any inclination to break into song. Fortunately for all concerned, the next day a servant took the top off the bottle to see what was inside. The sight of several big frogs so startled him that he ran off without replacing the cover; the frogs jumped out and presumably found their way back to the pond.

It became a habit with me to visit the pond on my own, in order to explore its banks and shallows. Taking off my shoes, I would wade into the muddy water tip to any knees, to pluck the water-lilies that floated on the surface.

One day I found the pond already occupied by several buffaloes. Their keeper, a boy a little older than me, was swimming about in the middle. Instead of climbing out on to the bank, he would pull himself up on the back of one of his buffaloes, stretch his naked brown body out on the animal's glistening wet hide and start singing to himself.

When he saw me staring at him from across the pond, he smiled, showing gleaming white teeth in a dark, sun-burnished face. He invited me to join him in a swim. I told him I couldn't swim, and he offered to teach me. I hesitated, knowing that Grandmother held strict and old-fashioned views about mixing with village children; but, deciding that Grandfather—who sometimes smoked a hookah on the sly—would get me out of any trouble that might occur, I took the bold step of accepting the boy's offer. Once taken, the step did not seem so bold.

He dived off the back of his buffalo, and swam across to

me. And I, having removed my clothes, followed his instructions until I was floundering about among the water-lilies. His name was Ramu, and he promised to give me swimming lessons every afternoon; and so it was during the afternoons—especially summer afternoons when everyone was asleep—that we usually met. Before long I was able to swim across the pond to sit with Ramu astride a contented buffalo, the great beast standing like an island in the middle of a muddy ocean.

Sometimes we would try racing the buffaloes, Ramu and I sitting on different mounts. But they were lazy creatures, and would leave one comfortable spot only to look for another; or, if they were in no mood for games, would roll over on their backs, taking us with them into the mud and green slime of the pond. Emerging in shades of green and khaki, I would slip into the house through the bathroom, bathing under the tap before getting into my clothes.

One afternoon, Ramu and I found a small tortoise in the mud, sitting over a hole in which it had laid several eggs. Ramu kept the eggs for his dinner, and I presented the tortoise to Grandfather. He had a weakness for tortoises, and was pleased with this addition to his menagerie, giving it a large tub of water all to itself, with an island of rocks in the middle. The tortoise, however, was always getting out of the tub and wandering about the house. As it seemed able to look after itself quite well, we did not interfere. If one of the dogs bothered it too much, it would draw its head and legs into its shell, and defy all their attempts at rough play.

Ramu came from a family of bonded labourers, and had received no schooling. But he was well-versed in folklore, and knew a great deal about birds and animals.

'Many birds are sacred,' said Ramu, as we watched a bluejay swoop down from a peepul tree and carry off a grasshopper. He told me that both the bluejay and Lord Shiva were called 'Nilkanth'. Shiva had a blue throat, like the bird, because out of compassion for the human race he had swallowed a deadly poison which was intended to destroy the world. Keeping the poison in his throat, he did not let it go any further.

'Are squirrels sacred?' I asked, seeing one sprint down the trunk of the peepul tree.

'Oh yes, Lord Krishna loved squirrels,' said Ramu. 'He would take them in his arms and stroke them with his long fingers. That is why they have four dark lines down their backs from head to tail. Krishna was very dark, and the lines are the marks of his fingers.

Both Ramu and Grandfather were of the opinion that we should be more gentle with birds and animals, and should not kill so many of them.

'It is also important that we respect them,' said Grandfather. 'We must acknowledge their rights. Everywhere, birds and animals are finding it more difficult to survive, because we are trying to destroy both them and their forests. They have to keep moving as the trees disappear.'

This was especially true of the forests near Dehra, where the tiger and the pheasant and the spotted deer were beginning to disappear.

Ramu and I spent many long summer afternoons at the pond. I still remember him with affection, though we never saw each other again after I left Dehra. He could not read or write, so we were unable to keep in touch. And neither his people, nor mine, knew of our friendship. The buffaloes and frogs had been our only confidants. They had accepted us as part of their own world, their muddy but comfortable pond. And when I left Dehra, both they and Ramu must have assumed that I would return again like the birds.

BIRDSONG IN THE HILLS

Bird-watching is more difficult in the hills than on the plains. Many birds are difficult to spot against the dark green of the trees or the varying shades of the hillsides. Large gardens and open fields make bird-watching much easier on the plains; but up here in the mountains one has to be quick of eye to spot a flycatcher flitting from tree to tree, or a mottled brown treecreeper ascending the trunk of oak or spruce. But few birds remain silent, and one learns of their presence from their calls or songs. Birdsong is with you wherever you go in the hills, from the foothills to the tree line; and it is often easier to recognize a bird from its voice than from its colourful but brief appearance.

The barbet is one of those birds which are heard more than they are seen. Summer visitors to our hill stations must have heard their monotonous, far-reaching call, *pee-oh, pee-oh,* or *un-nee-ow, un-nee-ow.* They would probably not have seen the birds, as they keep to the tops of high trees where they are not easily distinguished from the foliage. Apart from that, the sound carries for about half a mile, and as the bird has the habit of turning its head from side to side while calling, it is very difficult to know in which direction to look for it.

Barbets love listening to their own voices and often two or three birds answer each other from different trees, each trying to outdo the other in a shrill shouting match. Most birds are noisy during the mating season. Barbets are noisy all the year round!

Some people like the barbet's call and consider it both striking and pleasant. Some don't like it and simply consider it striking!

In parts of the Garhwal Himalayas, there is a legend that the bird is the reincarnation of a moneylender who died of grief at the unjust termination of a law suit. Eternally his plaint rises to heaven, *un-nee-ow, un-nee-ow!* which means, 'injustice, injustice'.

Barbets are found throughout the tropical world, but probably the finest of these birds is the Great Himalayan Barbet. Just over a foot in length, it has a massive yellow bill, almost as large as that of a toucan. The head and neck are a rich violet; the upper back is olive brown with pale green streaks. The wings are green, washed with blue, brown and yellow. In spite of all these brilliant colours, the barbet is not easily distinguished from its leafy surroundings. It goes for the highest treetops and seldom comes down to earth.

Hodgson's Grey-Headed Flycatcher-Warbler is the long name that ornithologists, in their infinite wisdom, have given to a very small bird. This tiny bird is heard, if not seen, more often than any other bird throughout the Western Himalayas. It is almost impossible to visit any hill station between Nainital and Dalhousie without noticing this warbler; its voice is heard in every second tree; and yet there are few who can say what it looks like.

Its song (if you can call it that) is not very musical, and Douglas Dewar in writing about it was reminded of a notice that once appeared in a third-rate music hall: the audience is respectfully requested not to throw things at the pianist. He is doing his best.

Our little warbler does his best, incessantly emitting four or five unmusical but joyful and penetrating notes.

He is much smaller than a sparrow, being only some four inches in length, of which one-third consists of tail. His lower plumage is bright yellow, his upper parts olive green; the head and neck are grey, the head being set off by cream-coloured eyebrows. He is an active little bird always on the move, and both he and his mate, and sometimes a few friends, hop about from leaf to leaf, looking for insects both large and small. And the way he puts away an inch long caterpillar would please the most accomplished spaghetti eater!

Another tiny bird more often than it is seen is the Green-Backed Tit, a smart little bird about the size of a sparrow. It constantly utters a sharp, rather metallic but not unpleasant, call which sounds like 'kiss me, kiss me, kiss me...'

Another fine singer is the sunbird, which is found in Kumaon and Garhwal. But perhaps the finest songster is the Grey-Winged Ouzel. Throughout the early summer he makes the wooded hillsides ring with his blackbird-like melody. The hill people call this bird the Kastura or Kasturi, a name also applied to the Himalayan Whistling Thrush. But the whistling thrush has a yellow bill, whereas the ouzel is red-billed and is much the sweeter singer.

Nightjars (or goatsuckers, to give them their ancient name) are birds that lie concealed during the day in shady woods, coming out at dusk on silent wings to hunt for insects. The nightjar has a huge frog-like mouth, but is best recognized by its long tail and wings and its curiously silent flight. After dusk and just before dawn, you can hear its curious call, *tonk-tonk, tonk-tonk*—a note like that produced by striking a plank with a hammer.

As we pass from the plains to the hills, the traveller is transported from one bird realm to another.

Rajpur is separated from Mussoorie by a five-mile footpath, and within that brief distance we find the caw of the house crow replaced by the deeper note of the corby. Instead of the crescendo shriek of the koel, the double note of the cuckoo meets the ear. For the eternal cooing of the little brown dove, the melodious kokla green pigeon is substituted. The harsh cries of the rose-ringed parakeets give place to the softer call of the slate-headed species. The dissonant voices of the seven sisters no longer issue from the bushes; their place is taken by the weird but more pleasing calls of the Himalayan streaked laughing thrushes.

When I first came to live in the hills, it was the song of the Himalayan Whistling Thrush that caught my attention. I did not see the bird that day. It kept to the deep shadows of the ravine below the old stone cottage.

The following day I was sitting at my window, gazing out at the new leaves on the walnut and wild pear trees. All was still, the wind was at peace with itself, the mountains brooded massively under the darkening sky. And then, emerging from the depths of that sunless chasm like a dark sweet secret, came the indescribably beautiful call of the whistling thrush.

It is a song that never fails to thrill and enchant me. The bird starts with a hesitant schoolboy whistle, as though trying out the tune; then, confident of the melody, it bursts into full song, a crescendo of sweet notes and variations that ring clearly across the hillside. Suddenly the song breaks off right in the middle of a cadenza, and I am left wondering what happened to make the bird stop so suddenly.

At first the bird was heard but never seen. Then one day I found the whistling thrush perched on the broken garden fence. He was deep glistening purple, his shoulders flecked with white; he has sturdy black legs and a strong yellow beak. A dapper fellow who would have looked just right in a top hat! When he saw me coming down the path, he uttered a sharp *kree-ee*—unexpectedly harsh when compared to his singing—and flew off into the shadowed ravine.

As the months passed, he grew used to my presence and became less shy. Once the rain water pipes were blocked, and this resulted in an overflow of water and a small permanent puddle under the steps. This became the whistling thrush's favourite bathing place. On sultry summer afternoons, while I was taking a siesta upstairs, I would hear the bird flapping about in the rainwater pool. A little later, refreshed and sunning himself on the roof, he would treat me to a little concert—performed, I could not help feeling, especially for my benefit.

It was Govind, the milkman, who told me the legend of the whistling thrush, locally called Kastura by the hill people, but also going by the name of Krishan-patti.

According to the story, Lord Krishna fell asleep near a mountain stream and while he slept, a small boy made off with the god's famous flute. Upon waking and finding his flute gone, Krishna was so angry that he changed the culprit into a bird. But having once played on the flute, the bird had learnt bits and pieces of Krishna's wonderful music. And so he continued, in his disrespectful way, to play the music of the gods, only stopping now and then (as the whistling thrush does) when he couldn't remember the tune.

It wasn't long before my whistling thrush was joined by a

female, who looked exactly like him. (I am sure there are subtle points of difference, but not to my myopic eyes!) Sometimes they gave solo performances, sometimes they sang duets; and these, no doubt, were love calls, because it wasn't long before the pair were making forays into the rocky ledges of the ravine, looking for a suitable maternity home. But a few breeding seasons were to pass before I saw any of their young.

After almost three years in the hills, I came to the conclusion that these were 'birds for all seasons'. They were liveliest in midsummer; but even in the depths of winter, with snow lying on the ground, they would suddenly start singing, as they flitted from pine to oak to naked chestnut.

As I write, there is a strong wind rushing through the trees and bustling about in the chimney, while distant thunder threatens a storm. Undismayed, the whistling thrushes are calling to each other as they roam the wind-threshed forest.

Whistling thrushes usually nest on rocky ledges near water; but my overtures of friendship may have given my visitors other ideas. Recently, I was away from Mussoorie for about a fortnight. When I returned, I was about to open the window when I noticed a large bundle of ferns, lichen, grass, mud and moss balanced outside on the window ledge. Peering through the glass, I was able to recognize this untidy bundle as a nest.

It meant, of course, that I couldn't open the window, as this would have resulted in the nest toppling over the edge. Fortunately the room had another window and I kept this one open to let in sunshine, fresh air, the music of birds and, always welcome, the call of the postman! The postman's call may not be as musical as birdsong, but this writer never tires of it, for it heralds the arrival of the occasional cheque that makes it possible for him to live close to nature.

And now, this very day, three pink freckled eggs lie in the cup of moss that forms the nursery in this jumble of a nest. The parent birds, both male and female, come and go, bustling about very efficiently, fully prepared for a great day that's coming soon.

The wild cherry trees, which I grew especially for birds, attract a great many small birds, both when it is in flower and when it is in fruit.

When it is covered with pale pink blossoms, the most common visitor is a little yellow-backed sunbird, who emits a squeaky little song as he flits from branch to branch. He extracts the nectar from the blossoms with his tubular tongue, sometimes while hovering on the wing but usually while clinging to the slender twigs.

Just as some vegetarians will occasionally condescend to eat meat, the sunbird (like the barbet) will vary his diet with insects. Small spiders, caterpillars, beetles, bugs and flies (probably in most cases themselves visitors to these flowers), fall prey to these birds. I have also seen a sunbird flying up and catching insects on the wing.

The flycatchers are gorgeous birds, especially the Paradise Flycatcher with its long white tail and ghost-like flight; and although they are largely insectivorous, like some meat-eaters they will also take a little fruit! And so they will occasionally visit the cherry tree when its sour little cherries are ripening. While travelling over the boughs, they utter twittering notes with occasional louder calls, and now and then the male bird breaks out into a sweet little song, thus justifying the name of Shah Bulbul by which he is known in northern India.

THE TUNNEL

It was almost noon, and the jungle was very still, very silent. Heat waves shimmered along the railway embankment where it cut a path through the tall evergreen trees. The railway lines were two straight black serpents disappearing into the tunnel in the hillside.

Suraj stood near the cutting, waiting for the midday train. It wasn't a station, and he wasn't catching a train. He was waiting so that he could watch the steam engine come roaring out of the tunnel.

He had cycled out of the town and taken the jungle path until he had come to a small village. He had left the cycle there, and walked over a low, scrub-covered hill and down to the tunnel exit.

Now he looked up. He had heard, in the distance, the shrill whistle of the engine. He couldn't see anything, because the train was approaching from the other side of the hill; but presently a sound like distant thunder issued from the tunnel, and he knew the train was coming through.

A second or two later, the steam engine shot out of the tunnel, snorting and puffing like some green, black and gold dragon, some beautiful monster out of Suraj's dreams. Showering sparks left and right, it roared a challenge to the jungle.

Instinctively, Suraj stepped back a few paces. And then the train had gone, leaving only a plume of smoke to drift lazily over tall shisham trees.

The jungle was still again. No one moved. Suraj turned from his contemplation of the drifting smoke and began walking along the embankment towards the tunnel.

The tunnel grew darker as he walked further into it. When he had gone about twenty yards, it became pitch black. Suraj had to turn and look back at the opening to reassure himself that there was still daylight outside. Ahead of him, the tunnel's other opening was just a small round circle of light.

The tunnel was still full of smoke from the train, but it would be several hours before another train came through. Till then, it belonged to the jungle again.

Suraj didn't stop, because there was nothing to do in the tunnel and nothing to see. He had simply wanted to walk through, so that he would know what the inside of a tunnel was really like. The walls were damp and sticky. A bat flew past. A lizard scuttled between the lines.

Coming straight from the darkness into the light, Suraj was dazzled by the sudden glare. He put a hand up to shade his eyes and looked up at the tree-covered hillside. He thought he saw something moving between the trees.

It was just a flash of orange and gold, and a long swishing tail. It was there between the trees for a second or two, and then it was gone.

About fifty feet from the entrance to the tunnel stood the watchman's hut. Marigolds grew in front of the hut, and at the back there was a small vegetable patch. It was the watchman's duty to inspect the tunnel and keep it clear of obstacles. Every day, before the train came through, he would walk the length of the tunnel. If all was well, he would return to his hut and take a nap. If something was wrong, he would walk back up the line and wave a red flag and the engine-driver would slow down. At night, the watchman lit an oil lamp and made a similar inspection of the tunnel. Of course, he could not stop the train if there was a porcupine on the line. But if there was any danger to the train, he'd go back up the line and wave his lamp to the approaching engine. If all was well, he'd hang his lamp at the door of the hut and go to sleep.

He was just settling down on his cot for an afternoon nap when he saw the boy emerge from the tunnel. He waited until Suraj was only a few feet away and then said, 'Welcome, welcome, I don't often have visitors. Sit down for a while, and tell me why you were inspecting my tunnel.'

'Is it your tunnel?' asked Suraj.

'It is,' said the watchman. 'It is truly my tunnel, since no one else will have anything to do with it. I have only lent it to the government.'

Suraj sat down on the edge of the cot.

'I wanted to see the train come through,' he said. 'And then, when it had gone, I thought I'd walk through the tunnel.'

'And what did you find in it?'

'Nothing. It was very dark. But when I came out, I thought I saw an animal—up on the hill—but I'm not sure, it moved away very quickly.'

'It was a leopard you saw,' said the watchman. 'My leopard.'

'Do you own a leopard too?'

'I do.'

'And do you lend it to the government?'

'I do not.'

'Is it dangerous?'

'No, it's a leopard that minds its own business. It comes to this range for a few days every month.'

'Have you been here a long time?' asked Suraj.

'Many years. My name is Sunder Singh.'

'My name's Suraj.'

'There's one train during the day. And another during the night. Have you seen the night mail come through the tunnel?'

'No. At what time does it come?'

'About nine o'clock, if it isn't late. You could come and sit here with me, if you like. And after it has gone, I'll take you home.'

'I shall ask my parents,' said Suraj. 'Will it be safe?'

'Of course. It's safer in the jungle than in the town. Nothing happens to me out here, but last month when I went into the town, I was almost run over by a bus.'

Sunder Singh yawned and stretched himself out on the cot. 'And now I'm going to take a nap, my friend. It is too hot to be up and about in the afternoon.'

'Everyone goes to sleep in the afternoon,' complained Suraj. 'My father lies down as soon as he's had his lunch.'

'Well, the animals also rest in the heat of the day. It is only the tribe of boys who cannot, or will not, rest.'

Sunder Singh placed a large banana leaf over his face to keep away the flies, and was soon snoring gently. Suraj stood up, looking up and down the railway tracks. Then he began walking back to the village.

The following evening, towards dusk, as the flying foxes swooped silently out of the trees, Suraj made his way to the watchman's hut.

It had been a long hot day, but now the earth was cooling, and a light breeze was moving through the trees. It carried with it a scent of mango blossoms, the promise of rain.

Sunder Singh was waiting for Suraj. He had watered his small garden, and the flowers looked cool and fresh. A kettle was boiling on a small oil stove.

'I'm making tea,' he said. 'There's nothing like a glass of hot tea while waiting for a train.'

They drank their tea, listening to the sharp notes of the tailorbird and the noisy chatter of the seven sisters. As the brief twilight faded, most of the birds fell silent. Sunder Singh lit his oil lamp and said it was time for him to inspect the tunnel. He moved off towards the tunnel, while Suraj sat on the cot, sipping his tea. In the dark, the trees seemed to move closer to him. And the night life of the forest was conveyed on the breeze—the sharp call of a barking deer, the cry of a fox, the quaint *tonk-tonk* of a nightjar. There were some sounds that Suraj couldn't recognize—sounds that came from the trees, creakings and whisperings, as though the trees were coming alive, stretching their limbs in the dark, shifting a little, flexing their fingers.

Sunder Singh stood inside the tunnel, trimming his lamp. The night sounds were familiar to him and he did not give them much thought; but something else—a padded footfall, a rustle of dry leaves—made him stand alert for a few seconds, peering into the darkness. Then, humming softly to himself, he returned to where Suraj was waiting. Another ten minutes remained for the night mail to arrive.

As Sunder Singh sat down on the cot beside Suraj, a new sound reached both of them quite distinctly—a rhythmic sawing sound, as if someone was cutting through the branch of a tree.

'What's that?' whispered Suraj.

'It's the leopard,' said Sunder Singh. 'I think it's in the tunnel.'

'The train will soon be here,' reminded Suraj.

'Yes, my friend. And if we don't drive the leopard out of the tunnel, it will be run over and killed. I can't let that happen.'

'But won't it attack us if we try to drive it out?' asked Suraj, beginning to share the watchman's concern.

'Not this leopard. It knows me well. We have seen each other many times. It has a weakness for goats and stray dogs, but it won't harm us. Even so, I'll take my axe with me. You stay here, Suraj.'

'No, I'm going with you. It'll be better than sitting here alone in the dark!'

'All right, but stay close behind me. And remember, there's nothing to fear.'

Raising his lamp high, Sunder Singh advanced into the tunnel, shouting at the top of his voice to try and scare away the animal. Suraj followed close behind, but he found he was unable to do any shouting. His throat was quite dry.

They had gone just about twenty paces into the tunnel when the light from the lamp fell upon the leopard. It was crouching between the tracks, only fifteen feet away from them. It was not a very big leopard, but it looked lithe and sinewy. Baring its teeth and snarling, it went down on its belly, tail twitching.

Suraj and Sunder Singh both shouted together. Their voices rang through the tunnel. And the leopard, uncertain as to how many terrifying humans were there in the tunnel with him, turned swiftly and disappeared into the darkness.

To make sure that it had gone, Sunder Singh and Suraj walked the length of the tunnel. When they returned to the entrance, the rails were beginning to hum. They knew the train was coming.

Suraj put his hand to the rails and felt its tremor. He heard the distant rumble of the train. And then the engine came round the bend, hissing at them, scattering sparks into the darkness, defying the jungle as it roared through the steep sides of the cutting. It charged straight at the tunnel, and into it, thundering past Suraj like the beautiful dragon of his dreams.

And when it had gone, the silence returned and the forest seemed to breathe, to live again. Only the rails still trembled with the passing of the train.

And they trembled to the passing of the same train, almost a week later, when Suraj and his father were both travelling in it.

Suraj's father was scribbling in a notebook, doing his accounts. Suraj sat at an open window staring out at the darkness. His father was going to Delhi on a business trip and had decided to take the boy along. 'I don't know where he gets to most of the time,' he'd complained. 'I think it's time he learnt something about my business.'

The night mail rushed through the forest with its hundreds of passengers. Tiny flickering lights came and went, as they passed small villages on the fringe of the jungle.

Suraj heard the rumble as the train passed over a small bridge. It was too dark to see the hut near the cutting, but he knew they must be approaching the tunnel. He strained his eyes looking out into the night; and then, just as the engine let out a shrill whistle, Suraj saw the lamp.

He couldn't see Sunder Singh, but he saw the lamp, and he knew that his friend was out there.

The train went into the tunnel and out again; it left the jungle behind and thundered across the endless plains; and Suraj stared out at the darkness, thinking of the lonely cutting in the forest, and the watchman with the lamp who would always remain a firefly for those travelling thousands, as he lit up the darkness for steam engines and leopards.

ESCAPE FROM JAVA

'No one, it seemed, was interested in defending Java, only in getting out as fast as possible.'

It all happened within the space of a few days. The cassia tree had barely come into flower when the first bombs fell on Batavia (now called Jakarta) and the bright pink blossoms lay scattered over the wreckage in the streets.

News had reached us that Singapore had fallen to the Japanese. My father said: 'I expect it won't be long before they take Java. With the British defeated, how can the Dutch be expected to win?' He did not mean to be critical of the Dutch; he knew they did not have the backing of an empire such as Britain then had. Singapore had been called the Gibraltar of the East. After its surrender there could only be retreat, a vast exodus of Europeans from Southeast Asia.

It was World War II. What the Javanese thought about the war is now hard for me to say, because I was only nine at the time and knew little of worldly matters. Most people knew they would be exchanging their Dutch-rulers for Japanese rulers; but there were also many who spoke in terms of freedom for Java when the war was over.

Our neighbor, Mr Hartono, was one of those who looked

ahead to a time when Java, Sumatra and the other islands would make up one independent nation. He was a college professor and spoke Dutch, Chinese, Javanese and a little English. His son, Sono, was about my age. He was the only boy I knew who could talk to me in English, and as a result we spent a lot of time together. Our favourite pastime was flying kites in the park.

The bombing soon put an end to kite flying. Air raid alerts sounded at all hours of the day and night, and although in the beginning most of the bombs fell near the docks, a couple of miles from where we lived, we had to stay indoors. If the planes sounded very near, we dived under beds or tables. I don't remember if there were any trenches. Probably there hadn't been time for trench digging, and now there was time only for digging graves. Events had moved all too swiftly, and everyone (except, of course, the Javanese) was anxious to get away from Java.

'When are you going?' asked Sono, as we sat on the verandah steps in a pause between air raids.

'I don't know,' I said. 'It all depends on my father.'

'My father says the Japs will be here in a week. And if you're still here then, they'll put you to work building a railway.'

'I wouldn't mind building a railway,' I said.

'But they won't give you enough to eat. Just rice with worms in it. And if you don't work properly they'll shoot you.'

'They do that to soldiers,' I said. 'We're civilians.'

'They do it to civilians, too,' said Sono.

What were my father and I doing in Batavia, when our home had been first in India and then in Singapore? He worked for a firm dealing in rubber, and six months earlier he had been sent to Batavia to open a new office in partnership with a Dutch business house. Although I was so young, I accompanied my father almost everywhere. My mother had died when I was very small, and my father had always looked after me. After the war was over, he was going to take me to England.

'Are we going to win the war?' I asked.

'It doesn't look it from here,' he said.

No, it didn't look as though we were winning. Standing at the docks with my father, I watched the ships arrive from Singapore, crowded with refugees—men, women and children all living on the decks in the hot tropical sun; they looked pale and worn out and worried. They were on their way to Colombo or Bombay. No one came ashore at Batavia. It wasn't British territory; it was Dutch, and everyone knew it wouldn't be Dutch for long.

'Aren't we going too?' I asked. 'Sono's father says the Japs will be here any day.'

'We've still got a few days,' said my father. He was a short, stocky man who seldom got excited. If he was worried, he didn't show it. 'I've got to wind up a few business matters, and then we'll be off.'

'How will we go? There's no room for us on those ships.'

'There certainly isn't. But we'll find a way, lad, don't worry.'

I didn't worry. I had complete confidence in my father's ability to find a way out of difficulties. He used to say, 'Every problem has a solution hidden away somewhere, and if only you look hard enough you will find it.'

There were British soldiers in the streets but they did not make us feel much safer. They were just waiting for troop ships to come and take them away. No one, it seemed, was interested in defending Java, only in getting out as fast as possible.

Although the Dutch were unpopular with the Javanese

people, there was no ill-feeling against individual Europeans. I could walk safely through the streets. Occasionally, small boys in the crowded Chinese quarter would point at me and shout, *'Orang Balandi!'* (Dutchman!) but they did so in good humour, and I didn't know the language well enough to stop and explain that the English weren't Dutch. For them, all white people were the same, and understandably so.

My father's office was in the commercial area, along the canal banks. Our two-storied house, about a mile away, was an old building with a roof of red tiles and a broad balcony which had stone dragons at either end. There were flowers in the garden almost all year round. If there was anything in Batavia more regular than the bombing, it was the rain, which came pattering down on the roof and on the banana fronds almost every afternoon. In the hot and steamy atmosphere of Java, the rain was always welcome.

There were no anti-aircraft guns in Batavia—at least we never heard any—and the Jap bombers came over at will, dropping their bombs by daylight. Sometimes bombs fell in the town. One day the building next to my father's office received a direct hit and tumbled into the river. A number of office workers were killed.

One day Sono said, 'The bombs are falling on Batavia, not in the countryside. Why don't we get cycles and ride out of town?'

I fell in with the idea at once. After the morning all-clear had sounded, we mounted our cycles and rode out of town. Mine was a hired cycle, but Sono's was his own. He'd had it since the age of five, and it was constantly in need of repairs. 'The soul has gone out of it,' he used to say.

Our fathers were at work; Sono's mother had gone out to

do her shopping (during air raids she took shelter under the most convenient shop counter) and wouldn't be back for at least an hour. We expected to be back before lunch.

We were soon out of town, on a road that passed through rice fields, pineapple orchards and cinchona plantations. On our right lay dark green hills; on our left, groves of coconut palms, and beyond them, the sea. Men and women were working in the rice fields, knee-deep in mud, their broad-brimmed hats protecting them from the fierce sun. Here and there a buffalo wallowed in a pool of brown water, while a naked boy lay stretched out on the animal's broad back.

We took a bumpy track through the palms. They grew right down to the edge of the sea. Leaving our cycles on the shingle, we ran down a smooth, sandy beach and into the shallow water.

'Don't go too far in,' warned Sono. 'There may be sharks about.'

Wading in amongst the rocks, we searched for interesting shells, then sat down on a large rock and looked out to sea, where a sailing ship moved placidly on the crisp blue waters. It was difficult to imagine that half the world was at war, and that Batavia, two or three miles away, was right in the middle of it.

On our way home we decided to take a shortcut through the rice fields, but soon found that our tires got bogged down in the soft mud. This delayed our return; and to make things worse, we got the roads mixed up and reached an area of the town that seemed unfamiliar. We had barely entered the outskirts when the siren sounded, to be followed soon after by the drone of approaching aircraft.

'Should we get off our cycles and take shelter somewhere?' I called out.

'No, let's race home!' shouted Sono. 'The bombs won't fall here.'

But he was wrong. The planes flew in very low. Looking up for a moment, I saw the sun blotted out by the sinister shape of a Jap fighter-bomber. We pedalled furiously, but we had barely covered fifty yards when there was a terrific explosion on our right, behind some houses. The shock sent us spinning across the road. We were flung from our cycles. And the cycles, still propelled by the blast, crashed into a wall.

I felt a stinging sensation in my hands and legs, as though scores of little insects had bitten me. Tiny droplets of blood appeared here and there on my flesh. Sono was on all fours, crawling beside me, and I saw that he too had the same small scratches on his hands and forehead, made by tiny shards of flying glass.

We were quickly on our feet, and then we began running in the general direction of our homes. The twisted cycles lay forgotten in the road.

'Get off the street, you two!' shouted someone from a window; but we weren't going to stop running until we got home. And we ran faster than we'd ever run in our lives.

My father and Sono's parents were themselves running about the street, calling for us, when we came rushing around the corner and tumbled into their arms.

'Where have you been?'

'What happened to you?'

'How did you get those cuts?'

All superfluous questions; but before we could recover our breath and start explaining, we were bundled into our respective homes. My father washed my cuts and scratches, dabbed at my face and legs with iodine—ignoring my yelps—and then stuck plaster all over my face.

Sono and I had both had a fright, and we did not venture far from the house again.

That night my father said, 'I think we'll able to leave in a day or two.'

'Has another ship come in?'

'No.'

'Then how are we going? By plane?'

'Wait and see, lad. It isn't settled yet. But we won't be able to take much with us—just enough to fill a couple of travelling bags.'

'What about the stamp collection?' I asked.

My father's stamp collection was quite valuable, and filled several volumes.

'I'm afraid we'll have to leave most of it behind,' he said. 'Perhaps Mr Hartono will keep it for me, and when the war is over—if it's ever over—we'll come back for it.'

'But we can take one or two albums with us, can't we?'

'I'll take one. There'll be room for one. Then if we're short on money in Bombay, we can sell the stamps.'

'Bombay? That's in India. I thought we were going back to England.'

'First we must go to India.'

The following morning I found Sono in the garden, patched up like me, and with one foot in a bandage. But he was as cheerful as ever and gave me his usual wide grin.

'We're leaving tomorrow,' I said.

The grin left his face.

'I will be sad when you go,' he said. 'But I will be glad,

too, because then you will be able to escape from the Japs.'

'After the war, I'll come back.'

'Yes, you must come back. And then, when we are big, we will go round the world together. I want to see England and America and Africa and India and Japan. I want to go everywhere.'

'We can't go everywhere.'

'Yes, we can. No one can stop us!'

We had to be up very early the next morning. Our bags had been packed late at night. We were taking a few clothes, some of my father's business papers, a pair of binoculars, one stamp album, and several bars of chocolate. I was pleased about the stamp album and the chocolates, but I had to give up several of my treasures—favourite books, the gramophone and records, an old Samurai sword, a train set and a dartboard. The only consolation was that Sono, and not a stranger, would have them.

In the first faint light of dawn a truck drew up in front of the house. It was driven by a Dutch businessman, Mr Hookens, who worked with my father. Sono was already at the gate, waiting to say goodbye.

'I have a present for you,' he said.

He took me by the hand and pressed a smooth, hard object into my palm. I grasped it and then held it up against the light. It was a beautiful little sea horse, carved out of pale blue jade.

'It will bring you luck,' said Sono.

'Thank you,' I said. 'I will keep it forever.'

And I slipped the little sea horse into my pocket.

'In you get, lad,' said my father, and I got up on the front seat between him and Mr Hookens.

As the truck started up, I turned to wave to Sono. He was sitting on his garden wall, grinning at me. He called out, 'We will go everywhere, and no one can stop us!'

He was still waving when the truck took us round the bend at the end of the road.

We drove through the still, quiet streets of Batavia, occasionally passing burnt-out trucks and shattered buildings. Then we left the sleeping city far behind and were climbing into the forested hills. It had rained during the night, and when the sun came up over the green hills, it twinkled and glittered on the broad, wet leaves. The light in the forest changed from dark green to greenish gold, broken here and there by the flaming red or orange of a trumpet-shaped blossom. It was impossible to know the names of all those fantastic plants! The road had been cut through dense tropical forest, and on either side, the trees jostled each other, hungry for the sun; but they were chained together by the liana creepers and vines that fed upon the same struggling trees.

Occasionally a Jelarang, a large Javan squirrel, frightened by the passing of the truck, leapt through the trees before disappearing into the depths of the forest. We saw many birds: peacocks, jungle fowl and once, standing majestically at the side of the road, a crowned pigeon, its great size and splendid crest making it a striking object even at a distance. Mr Hookens slowed down so that we could look at the bird. It bowed its head so that its crest swept the ground; then it emitted a low, hollow boom rather like the call of a turkey.

When we came to a small clearing, we stopped for breakfast. Butterflies—black, green and gold—flitted across the clearing. The silence of the forest was broken only by the drone of airplanes, Japanese Zeros heading for Batavia on another raid. I thought about Sono, and wondered what he would be doing at home: probably trying out the gramophone!

We ate boiled eggs and drank tea from a thermos, then got back into the truck and resumed our journey.

I must have dozed off soon after because the next thing I remember is that we were going quite fast down a steep, winding road, and in the distance I could see a calm blue lagoon.

'We've reached the sea again,' I said.

'That's right,' said my father. 'But we're now nearly a hundred miles from Batavia, in another part of the island. You're looking out over the Sunda Straits.'

Then he pointed towards a shimmering white object resting on the waters of the lagoon.

'There's our plane,' he said.

'A seaplane!' I exclaimed. 'I never guessed. Where will it take us?'

'To India, I hope. There aren't many other places left to go to!'

It was a very old seaplane, and no one, not even the captain—the pilot was called the captain—could promise that it would take off. Mr Hookens wasn't coming with us; he said the plane would be back for him the next day. Besides my father and me, there were four other passengers, and all but one were Dutch. The odd man out was a Londoner, a motor mechanic who'd been left behind in Java when his unit was evacuated. (He told us later that he'd fallen asleep at a bar in the Chinese quarter, waking up some hours after his regiment had moved off!) He looked rather scruffy. He'd lost the top button of his shirt, but instead of leaving his collar open, as we did, he'd kept it together with a large safety pin, which thrust itself out from behind a bright pink tie.

'It's a relief to find you here, guvnor,' he said, shaking my father by the hand. 'Knew you for a Yorkshireman the minute I set eyes on you. It's the *song fried* that does it, if you know what I mean.' (He meant *sang froid,* French for a 'cool look'.) 'And here I was, with all these flippin' forriners, and me not knowing a word of what they've been yattering about. Do you think this old tub will get us back to Blighty?'

'It does look a bit shaky,' said my father. 'One of the first flying boats, from the looks of it. If it gets us to Bombay, that's far enough.'

'Anywhere out of Java's good enough for me,' said our new companion. 'The name's Muggeridge.'

'Pleased to know you, Mr Muggeridge,' said my father. 'I'm Bond. This is my son.'

Mr Muggeridge rumpled my hair and favoured me with a large wink.

The captain of the seaplane was beckoning to us to join him in a small skiff which was about to take us across a short stretch of water to the seaplane.

'Here we go,' said Mr Muggeridge. 'Say your prayers and keep your fingers crossed.'

The seaplane was a long time getting airborne. It had to make several runs before it finally took off; then, lurching drunkenly, it rose into the clear blue sky.

'For a moment I thought we were going to end up in the briny,' said Mr Muggeridge, untying his seat belt. 'And talkin' of fish, I'd give a week's wages for a plate of fish an' chips and a pint of beer.'

'I'll buy you a beer in Calcutta,' said my father.

'Have an egg,' I said, remembering we still had some boiled eggs in one of the travelling bags.

'Thanks, mate,' said Mr Muggeridge, accepting an egg with alacrity. 'A real egg, too! I've been livin' on egg powder these last six months. That's what they give you in the army. And it ain't hens' eggs they make it from, let me tell you. It's either gulls' or turtles' eggs!'

'No,' said my father with a straight face. 'Snakes' eggs.'

Mr Muggeridge turned a delicate shade of green; but he soon recovered his poise, and for about an hour kept talking about almost everything under the sun, including Churchill, Hitler, Roosevelt, Mahatma Gandhi and Betty Grable. (The last-named was famous for her beautiful legs.) He would have gone on talking all the way to India had he been given a chance, but suddenly a shudder passed through the old plane, and it began lurching again.

'I think an engine is giving trouble,' said my father.

When I looked through the small glassed-in window, it seemed as though the sea was rushing up to meet us.

The co-pilot entered the passenger cabin and said something in Dutch. The passengers looked dismayed and immediately began fastening their seat belts.

'Well, what did the blighter say?' asked Mr Muggeridge.

'I think he's going to have to ditch the plane,' said my father, who knew enough Dutch to get the gist of anything that was said.

'Down in the drink!' exclaimed Mr Muggeridge. 'Gawd 'elp us! And how far are we from India, guv?'

'A few hundred miles,' said my father.

'Can you swim, mate?' asked Mr Muggeridge looking at me.

'Yes,' I said. 'But not all the way to Bombay. How far can you swim?'

'The length of a bathtub,' he said.

'Don't worry,' said my father. 'Just make sure your life jacket's properly tied.'

We looked to our life jackets; my father checked mine twice, making sure that it was properly fastened.

The pilot had now cut both engines, and was bringing the plane down in a circling movement. But he couldn't control the speed, and it was tilting heavily to one side. Instead of landing smoothly on its belly, it came down on a wing tip, and this caused the plane to swivel violently around in the choppy sea. There was a terrific jolt when the plane hit the water, and if it hadn't been for the seat belts, we'd have been flung from our seats. Even so, Mr Muggeridge struck his head against the seat in front, and he was now holding a bleeding nose and using some shocking language.

As soon as the plane came to a standstill, my father undid my seat belt. There was no time to lose. Water was already filling the cabin, and all the passengers—except one, who was dead in his seat with a broken neck—were scrambling for the exit hatch. The co-pilot pulled a lever and the door fell away to reveal high waves slapping against the sides of the stricken plane.

Holding me by the hand, my father was leading me towards the exit.

'Quick, lad,' he said. 'We won't stay afloat for long.'

'Give us a hand!' shouted Mr Muggeridge, still struggling with his life jacket. 'First this bloody bleedin' nose, and now something's gone and stuck.'

My father helped him fix the life jacket, then pushed him out of the door ahead of us.

As we swam away from the seaplane (Mr Muggeridge splashing furiously alongside us), we were aware of the other passengers in the water. One of them shouted to us in Dutch to follow him.

We swam after him towards the dinghy, which had been released the moment we hit the water. That yellow dinghy, bobbing about on the waves, was as welcome as land.

All who had left the plane managed to climb into the dinghy. We were seven altogether—a tight fit. We had hardly settled down in the well of the dinghy when Mr Muggeridge, still holding his nose, exclaimed, 'There she goes!' And as we looked on helplessly, the seaplane sank swiftly and silently beneath the waves.

The dinghy had shipped a lot of water, and soon everyone was busy bailing it out with mugs (there were a couple in the dinghy), hats and bare hands. There was a light swell, and every now and then water would roll in again and half fill the dinghy. But within half an hour, we had most of the water out, and then it was possible to take turns, two men doing the bailing while the others rested. No one expected me to do this work, but I took a hand anyway, using my father's sola-topee for the purpose.

'Where are we?' asked one of the passengers.

'A long way from anywhere,' said another.

'There must be a few islands in the Indian Ocean.'

'But we may be at sea for days before we come to one of them.'

'Days or even weeks,' said the captain. 'Let us look at our supplies.'

The dinghy appeared to be fairly well provided with emergency rations: biscuits, raisins, chocolates (we'd lost our own) and enough water to last a week. There was also a first-aid box, which was put to immediate use, as Mr Muggeridge's nose needed attention. A few others had cuts and bruises. One of the passengers had received a hard knock on the head and appeared to be suffering from loss of memory. He had no idea how we happened to be drifting about in the middle of the Indian Ocean; he was convinced that we were on a pleasure cruise a few miles off Batavia.

The unfamiliar motion of the dinghy, as it rose and fell in the troughs between the waves, resulted in almost everyone getting seasick. As no one could eat anything, a day's rations were saved.

The sun was very hot, but my father covered my head with a large spotted handkerchief. He'd always had a fancy for bandana handkerchiefs with yellow spots and seldom carried fewer than two on his person; so he had one for himself too. The sola topee, well soaked in seawater, was being used by Mr Muggeridge.

It was only when I had recovered to some extent from my seasickness that I remembered the valuable stamp album, and sat up, exclaiming, 'The stamps! Did you bring the stamp album, Dad?'

He shook his head ruefully. 'It must be at the bottom of the sea by now,' he said. 'But don't worry, I kept a few rare stamps in my wallet.' And looking pleased with himself, he tapped the pocket of his bush shirt.

The dinghy drifted all day, with no one having the least idea where it might be taking us.

'Probably going round in circles,' said Mr Muggeridge pessimistically.

There was no compass and no sail, and paddling wouldn't have got us far even if we'd had paddles; we could only resign ourselves to the whims of the current and hope it would take us towards land or at least to within hailing distance of some passing ship.

The sun went down like an overripe tomato dissolving slowly in the sea. The darkness pressed down on us. It was a moonless night, and all we could see was the white foam on the crests of the waves. I lay with my head on my father's shoulder, and looked up at the stars which glittered in the remote heavens.

'Perhaps your friend Sono will look up at the sky tonight and see those same stars,' said my father. 'The world isn't so big after all.'

'All the same, there's a lot of sea around us,' said Mr Muggeridge from out of the darkness.

Remembering Sono, I put my hand in my pocket and was reassured to feel the smooth outline of the jade seahorse.

'I've still got Sono's seahorse,' I said, showing it to my father.

'Keep it carefully,' he said. 'It may bring us luck.'

'Are seahorses lucky?'

'Who knows? But he gave it to you with love, and love is like a prayer. So keep it carefully.'

I didn't sleep much that night. I don't think anyone slept. No one spoke much either, except of course Mr Muggeridge, who kept muttering something about cold beer and salami.

I didn't feel so sick the next day. By ten o'clock I was quite hungry; but breakfast consisted of two biscuits, a piece of chocolate, and a little drinking water. It was another hot day, and we were soon very thirsty, but everyone agreed that we should ration ourselves strictly.

Two or three still felt ill, but the others, including Mr Muggeridge, had recovered their appetites and normal spirits, and there was some discussion about the prospects of being picked up.

'Are there any distress-rockets in the dinghy?' asked my father. 'If we see a ship or a plane, we can fire a rocket and hope to be spotted. Otherwise there's not much chance of our being seen from a distance.'

A thorough search was made in the dinghy, but there were no rockets.

'Someone must have used them last Guy Fawkes Day,' commented Mr Muggeridge.

'They don't celebrate Guy Fawkes Day in Holland,' said my father. 'Guy Fawkes was an Englishman.'

'Ah,' said Mr Muggeridge, not in the least put out. 'I've always said, most great men are Englishmen. And what did this chap Guy Fawkes do?'

'Tried to blow up Parliament,' said my father.

That afternoon we saw our first sharks. They were enormous creatures, and as they glided backward and forward under the boat it seemed they might hit and capsize us. They went away for some time, but returned in the evening.

At night, as I lay half asleep beside my father, I felt a few drops of water strike my face. At first I thought it was the seaspray; but when the sprinkling continued, I realized that it was raining lightly.

'Rain!' I shouted, sitting up. 'It's raining!'

Everyone woke up and did their best to collect water in mugs, hats or other containers. Mr Muggeridge lay back with his mouth open, drinking the rain as it fell.

'This is more like it,' he said. 'You can have all the sun an' sand in the world. Give me a rainy day in England!'

But by early morning the clouds had passed, and the day turned out to be even hotter than the previous one. Soon we were all red and raw from sunburn. By midday even Mr Muggeridge was silent. No one had the energy to talk.

Then my father whispered, 'Can you hear a plane, lad?'

I listened carefully, and above the hiss of the waves I heard what sounded like the distant drone of a plane; but it must have been very far away, because we could not see it. Perhaps it was flying into the sun, and the glare was too much for our sore eyes; or perhaps we'd just imagined the sound.

Then the Dutchman who'd lost his memory thought he saw land, and kept pointing towards the horizon and saying, 'That's Batavia, I told you we were close to shore!' No one else saw anything. So my father and I weren't the only ones imagining things.

Said my father, 'It only goes to show that a man can see what he wants to see, even if there's nothing to be seen!'

The sharks were still with us. Mr Muggeridge began to resent them. He took off one of his shoes and hurled it at the nearest shark; but the big fish ignored the shoe and swam on after us.

'Now, if your leg had been in that shoe, Mr Muggeridge, the shark might have accepted it,' observed my father.

'Don't throw your shoes away,' said the captain. 'We might land on a deserted coastline and have to walk hundreds of miles!'

A light breeze sprang up that evening, and the dinghy moved more swiftly on the choppy water.

'At last we're moving forward,' said the captain.

'In circles,' said Mr Muggeridge.

But the breeze was refreshing; it cooled our burning limbs and helped us to get some sleep. In the middle of the night, I woke up feeling very hungry.

'Are you all right?' asked my father, who had been awake all the time.

'Just hungry,' I said.

'And what would you like to eat?'

'Oranges!'

He laughed. 'No oranges on board. But I kept a piece of my chocolate for you. And there's a little water, if you're thirsty.'

I kept the chocolate in my mouth for a long time, trying to make it last. Then I sipped a little water.

'Aren't you hungry?' I asked.

'Ravenous! I could eat a whole turkey. When we get to Calcutta or Madras or Colombo, or wherever it is we get to, we'll go to the best restaurant in town and eat like—like—'

'Like shipwrecked sailors!' I said.

'Exactly.'

'Do you think we'll ever get to land, Dad?'

'I'm sure we will. You're not afraid, are you?'

'No. Not as long as you're with me.'

Next morning, to everyone's delight, we saw seagulls. This was a sure sign that land couldn't be far away; but a dinghy could take days to drift a distance of thirty or forty miles. The birds wheeled noisily above the dinghy. Their cries were the first familiar sounds we had heard for three days and three nights, apart from the wind and the sea and our own weary voices.

The sharks had disappeared, and that too was an encouraging sign. They didn't like the oil slicks that were appearing in the water.

But presently the gulls left us, and we feared we were drifting away from land.

'Circles,' repeated Mr Muggeridge. 'Circles.'

We had sufficient food and water for another week at sea; but no one even wanted to think about spending another week at sea.

The sun was a ball of fire. Our water ration wasn't sufficient to quench our thirst. By noon, we were without much hope or energy.

My father had his pipe in his mouth. He didn't have any tobacco, but he liked holding the pipe between his teeth. He said it prevented his mouth from getting too dry.

The sharks came back.

Mr Muggeridge removed his other shoe and threw it at them.

'Nothing like a lovely wet English summer,' he mumbled.

I fell asleep in the well of the dinghy, my father's large handkerchief spread over my face. The yellow spots on the cloth seemed to grow into enormous revolving suns.

When I woke up, I found a huge shadow hanging over us. At first I thought it was a cloud. But it was a shifting shadow. My father took the handkerchief from my face and said, 'You can wake up now, lad. We'll be home and dry soon.'

A fishing boat was beside us, and the shadow came from its wide flapping sail. A number of bronzed, smiling, chattering fishermen—Burmese, as we discovered later—were gazing down at us from the deck of their boat.

A few days later, my father and I were in Calcutta.

My father sold his rare stamps for over a thousand rupees, and we were able to live in a comfortable hotel. Mr Muggeridge was flown back to England. Later we got a postcard from him saying the English rain was awful!

'And what about us?' I asked. 'Aren't we going back to England?'

'Not yet,' said my father. 'You'll be going to a boarding school in Shimla until the war's over.'

'But why should I leave you?' I asked.

'Because I've joined the R.A.F.,' he said. 'Don't worry, I'm being posted in Delhi. I'll be able to come up to see you sometimes.'

A week later I was on a small train which went chugging up the steep mountain track to Shimla. Several Indian, Anglo-Indian and English children tumbled around in the compartment. I felt quite out of place among them, as though I had grown out of their pranks. But I wasn't unhappy. I knew my father would be coming to see me soon. He'd promised me some books, a pair of rollerskates and a cricket bat, just as soon as he got his first month's pay.

Meanwhile, I had the jade seahorse which Sono had given me.

And I have it with me today.

CROSSING THE ROAD

Samuel was a snail of some individuality. Some considered him to be the bad snail in the family, but that was because he did not listen to his elders but liked to do things in his own way, trying out new plants or venturing into forbidden places. Birds and butterflies recognized no man-made borders, so why should snails? They'd been around longer than humans and were likely to be around even longer.

Not that Samuel had any global ambitions. It was just that the cabbage patch in which he and his fellow snails had been living did not appeal to him any more. He was heartily sick of cabbage leaves. And just across a busy road—his international boundary—was a field full of delicious looking lettuce. And any snail would prefer lettuce to cabbage.

The trouble was, it was a very busy road, linking one city to another, and on it flowed a constant stream of cars, trucks, motorcycles, bicycles, vans, even the occasional steamroller. Samuel did not like the idea of being crushed under a steamroller. There were better ways of exiting planet Earth—being swallowed by a large stork, for instance.

And then, of course, snails can't run. With the help of a little of their own juices, they glide slowly and leisurely over grass and weed and pebbles, in search of a juicy leaf or the company of a fellow snail. They were not made to run. They are not predators like the larger carnivores. Nor do they prey on each other like humans. They are all for minding their own business. And now here was Samuel, making it his business to invade that lettuce patch on the other side of the road.

Well, nothing ventured nothing gained. And ignoring the warnings of friends and familiars, Samuel set out to cross that life-threatening road. He could, of course, have waited until it was dark, but the road would have been no safer then. A constant stream of container trucks came thundering down the highway all through the night.

Tentacles waving, he began his stately crawl across the road.

Almost immediately he was nearly run over by a boy on a bicycle. Instinctively, Samuel withdrew into his little shell. Not that it would have made any difference. It might have protected him from a small bird, but not from a cycle tyre.

Samuel looked up and down the road. It was a single width road, and vehicles could approach from either direction. It appeared to be clear at the moment.

Samuel advanced, covering a distance of some twelve inches in sixty seconds flat.

Then—*woosh*—a car sped by, its tyres missing Samuel by inches. He was almost blown away by a cloud of dust and exhaust fumes.

And then came another car. Samuel cringed. And survived. And wondered if he should turn around and go back the way he came. But snails aren't great thinkers. The lettuce patch was all that mattered.

Samuel had advanced by two or three feet when there came a deep rumbling sound and he felt the ground quiver beneath him. A huge truck was bearing down on him!

Sometimes it is an advantage to be small. Samuel was somewhere in the middle of the road, and nowhere near the wheels when the truck thundered over him. All the same he was dazed and shaken, unable to move any further. Soon another truck would be coming along. Or was it a tractor that was chugging along towards him?

Just then there was a squeal of brakes, a blare of horns, and a tremendous crash. The truck had hit an oncoming car and both had veered off the road and were lying in a ditch. For a time all traffic ceased. Samuel emitted a slimy jet and began to crawl again. Then there was a burst of activity.

A motorcycle came tearing down the road, whizzing past a bewildered Samuel, and then stopping at the accident site. A policeman dismounted. In the distance a siren wailed. An ambulance was on its way.

And then it began to rain, a gentle patter on the tarmac. Refreshed, Samuel slid forward. The rain came down harder, and a fallen peepul leaf came sailing towards Samuel. It stopped beside him and Samuel crawled to the leaf. A spurt of rainwater picked up the leaf and sent it sailing across the remainder of the road and onto the grass verge.

Excelsior!

Samuel was home if not dry.

The lettuce field stretched before him. Motor horns and ambulance sirens melted into the distance. Humans could take care of themselves. So could snails! It would take him weeks to munch his way through a small corner of that lettuce patch, but he was going to try. To the winner the spoils!

The rain stopped and he began his feast.

The lettuce was all right, but it wasn't much better than the cabbage field he had left a little over an hour ago. Had the journey been worthwhile? Could he cross that road again? The odds were against survival.

He'd just have to settle down in this new and unfamiliar world. The grass is always greener on the other side—until you get there!

THE EYES OF THE EAGLE

It was a high, piercing sound, almost like the yelping of a dog. Jai stopped picking the wild strawberries that grew in the grass around him, and looked up at the sky. He had a dog—a shaggy guard-dog called Motu—but Motu did not yet yelp, he growled and barked. The strange sound came from the sky, and Jai had heard it before. Now, realizing what it was, he jumped to his feet, calling to his dog, calling his sheep to start for home. Motu came bounding towards him, ready for a game.

'Not now, Motu!' said Jai. 'We must get the lambs home quickly.' Again he looked up at the sky.

He saw it now, a black speck against the sun, growing larger as it circled the mountain, coming lower every moment—a Golden Eagle, king of the skies over the higher Himalayas, ready now to swoop and seize its prey.

Had it seen a pheasant or a pine marten? Or was it after one of the lambs? Jai had never lost a lamb to an eagle, but recently some of the other shepherds had been talking about a golden eagle that had been preying on their flocks.

The sheep had wandered some way down the side of the mountain, and Jai ran after them to make sure that none of the lambs had gone off on its own.

Motu ran about, barking furiously. He wasn't very good at

keeping the sheep together—he was often bumping into them and sending them tumbling down the slope—but his size and bear-like look kept the leopards and wolves at a distance.

Jai was counting the lambs; they were bleating loudly and staying close to their mothers. *One—two—three—four...*

There should have been a fifth. Jai couldn't see it on the slope below him. He looked up towards a rocky ledge near the steep path to the Tung temple. The golden eagle was circling the rocks.

The bird disappeared from sight for a moment, then rose again with a small creature grasped firmly in its terrible talons.

'It has taken a lamb!' shouted Jai. He started scrambling up the slope. Motu ran ahead of him, barking furiously at the big bird as it glided away over the tops of the stunted junipers to its eyrie on the cliffs above Tung.

There was nothing that Jai and Motu could do except stare helplessly and angrily at the disappearing eagle. The lamb had died the instant it had been struck. The rest of the flock seemed unaware of what had happened. They still grazed on the thick, sweet grass of the mountain slopes.

'We had better drive them home, Motu,' said Jai, and at a nod from the boy, the big dog bounded down the slope, to take part in his favourite game of driving the sheep homewards. Soon he had them running all over the place, and Jai had to dash about trying to keep them together. Finally, they straggled homewards.

'A fine lamb gone,' said Jai to himself gloomily. 'I wonder what Grandfather will say.'

Grandfather said, 'Never mind. It had to happen some day. That eagle has been watching the sheep for some time.'

Grandmother, more practical, said; 'We could have sold the lamb for three hundred rupees. You'll have to be more careful in future, Jai. Don't fall asleep on the hillside, and don't read storybooks when you are supposed to be watching the sheep!'

'I wasn't reading this morning,' said Jai truthfully, forgetting to mention that he had been gathering strawberries.

'It's good for him to read,' said Grandfather, who had never had the luck to go to school. In his days, there weren't any schools in the mountains. Now there was one in every village.

'Time enough to read at night,' said Grandmother, who did not think much of the little one-room school down at Maku, their home village.

'Well, these are the October holidays,' said Grandfather. 'Otherwise he would not be here to help us with the sheep. It will snow by the end of the month, and then we will move with the flock. You will have more time for reading then, Jai.'

◆

At Maku, which was down in the warmer valley, Jai's parents tilled a few narrow terraces on which they grew barley, millets and potatoes. The old people brought their sheep up to the Tung meadows to graze during the summer months. They stayed in a small stone hut just off the path which pilgrims took to the ancient temple. At twelve thousand feet above sea level, it was the highest Hindu temple on the inner Himalayan ranges.

The following day Jai and Motu were very careful. The did not let the sheep out of sight even for a minute. Nor did they catch sight of the golden eagle. 'What if it attacks again?' wondered Jai. 'How will I stop it?'

The great eagle, with its powerful beak and talons, was more than a match for boy or dog. Its hind claw, four inches round the curve, was its most dangerous weapon. When it spread its wings, the distance from tip to tip was more than eight feet.

The eagle did not come that day because it had fed well and was now resting in its eyrie. Old bones, which had belonged to pheasants, snow-cocks, pine martens and even foxes, were scattered about the rocks which formed the eagle's home. The eagle had a mate, but it was not the breeding season and she was away on a scouting expedition of her own.

The golden eagle stood on its rocky ledge, staring majestically across the valley. Its hard, unblinking eyes missed nothing. Those strange orange-yellow eyes could spot a field-rat or a mouse-hare more than a hundred yards below.

There were other eagles on the mountain, but usually they kept to their own territory. And only the bolder ones went for lambs, because the flocks were always protected by men and dogs.

The eagle took off from its eyrie and glided gracefully, powerfully over the valley, circling the Tung mountain.

Below lay the old temple, built from slabs of grey granite. A line of pilgrims snaked up the steep, narrow path. On the meadows below the peak, the sheep grazed peacefully, unaware of the presence of the eagle. The great bird's shadow slid over the sunlit slopes.

The eagle saw the boy and the dog, but he did not fear them. He had his eye on a lamb that was frisking about on the grass, a few feet away from the other grazing sheep.

Jai did not see the eagle until it swept round an outcrop of rocks about a hundred feet away. It moved silently, without any movement of its wings, for it had already built up the momentum for its dive. Now it came straight at the lamb.

Motu saw the bird in time. With a low growl he dashed forward and reached the side of the lamb at almost the same instant that the eagle swept in.

There was a terrific collision. Feathers flew. The eagle screamed with rage. The lamb tumbled down the slope, and Motu howled in pain as the huge beak struck him high on the leg.

The big bird, a little stunned by the clash, flew off rather unsteadily, with a mighty beating of its wings.

Motu had saved the lamb. It was frightened but unhurt. Bleating loudly, it joined the other sheep, who took up the bleating. Jai ran up to Motu, who lay whimpering on the ground. There was no sign of the eagle. Quickly he removed his shirt and vest; then he wrapped his vest round the dog's wound, tying it in position with his belt.

Motu could not get up, and he was much too heavy for Jai to carry. Jai did not want to leave his dog alone, in case the eagle returned to attack.

He stood up, cupped his hand to his mouth, and began calling for his grandfather.

'Dada, dada!' he shouted, and presently Grandfather heard him and came stumbling down the slope. He was followed by another shepherd, and together they lifted Motu and carried him home.

Motu had a bad wound, but Grandmother cleaned it and applied a paste made of herbs. Then she laid strips of carrot over the wound—an old mountain remedy—and bandaged the leg. But it would be some time before Motu could run about again. By then it would probably be snowing and time to leave these high-altitude pastures and return to the valley. Meanwhile, the sheep had to be taken out to graze, and Grandfather decided to accompany Jai for the remaining period.

They did not see the golden eagle for two or three days, and, when they did, it was flying over the next range. Perhaps it had found some other source of food, or even another flock of sheep. 'Are you afraid of the eagle?' Grandfather asked Jai.

'I wasn't before,' said Jai. 'Not until it hurt Motu. I did not know it could be so dangerous. But Motu hurt it too. He banged straight into it!'

'Perhaps it won't bother us again,' said Grandfather thoughtfully. 'A bird's wing is easily injured—even an eagle's.'

Jai wasn't so sure. He had seen it strike twice, and he knew that it was not afraid of anyone. Only when it learnt to fear his presence would it keep away from the flock.

The next day Grandfather did not feel well; he was feverish and kept to his bed. Motu was hobbling about gamely on three legs; the wounded leg was still very sore.

'Don't go too far with the sheep,' said Grandmother. 'Let them graze near the house.'

'But there's hardly any grass here,' said Jai.

'I don't want you wandering off while that eagle is still around.'

'Give him my stick,' said Grandfather from his bed. Grandmother took it from the corner and handed it to the boy.

It was an old stick, made of wild cherrywood, which Grandfather often carried around. The wood was strong and well-seasoned; the stick was stout and long. It reached up to Jai's shoulders.

'Don't lose it,' said Grandfather. 'It was given to me many years ago by a wandering scholar who came to the Tung temple. I was going to give it to you when you got bigger, but perhaps this is the right time for you to have it. If the eagle comes near you, swing the stick around your head. That should frighten it off!'

Clouds had gathered over the mountains, and a heavy mist hid the Tung temple. With the approach of winter, the flow of pilgrims had been reduced to a trickle. The shepherds had started leaving the lush meadows and returning to their villages at lower altitudes. Very soon the bears and the leopards and the golden eagles would have the high ranges all to themselves.

Jai used the cherrywood stick to prod the sheep along the path until they reached the steep meadows. The stick would have to be a substitute for Motu. And they seemed to respond to it more readily than they did to Motu's mad charges.

Because of the sudden cold and the prospect of snow, Grandmother had made Jai wear a rough woollen jacket and a pair of high boots bought from a Tibetan trader. He wasn't used to the boots—he wore sandals at other times—and had some difficulty in climbing quickly up and down the hillside. It was tiring work, trying to keep the flock together. The cawing of some crows warned Jai that the eagle might be around, but the mist prevented him from seeing very far.

After some time the mist lifted and Jai was able to see the temple and the snow peaks towering behind it. He saw the golden eagle, too. It was circling high overhead. Jai kept close to the flock—one eye on the eagle, one eye on the restless sheep.

Then the great bird stooped and flew lower. It circled the temple and then pretended to go away. Jai felt sure it would be back. And a few minutes later it reappeared from the other side of the mountain. It was much lower now, wings spread out and back, taloned feet to the fore, piercing eyes fixed on its target—a small lamb that had suddenly gone frisking down the slope, away from Jai and the flock.

Now it flew lower still, only a few feet off the ground, paying no attention to the boy.

It passed Jai with a great rush of air, and as it did so the boy struck out with his stick and caught the bird a glancing blow.

The eagle missed its prey, and the tiny lamb skipped away.

To Jai's amazement, the bird did not fly off. Instead it landed on the hillside and glared at the boy, as a king would glare at a humble subject who had dared to pelt him with a pebble.

The golden eagle stood almost as tall as Jai. Its wings were still outspread. Its fierce eyes seemed to be looking through and through the boy.

Jai's first instinct was to turn and run. But the cherrywood stick was still in his hands, and he felt sure there was power in it. He saw that the eagle was about to launch itself again at the lamb. Instead of running away, he ran forward, the stick raised above his head.

The eagle rose a few feet off the ground and struck out with its huge claws.

Luckily for Jai, his heavy jacket took the force of the blow. A talon ripped through the sleeve, and the sleeve fell away. At the same time the heavy stick caught the eagle across its open wing. The bird gave a shrill cry of pain and fury. Then it turned and flapped heavily away, flying unsteadily because of its injured wing.

Jai still clutched the stick, because he expected the bird to return; he did not even glance at his torn jacket. But the golden eagle had alighted on a distant rock and was in no hurry to return to the attack.

Jai began driving the sheep home. The clouds had become heavy and black, and presently the first snowflakes began to fall.

Jai saw a hare go lolloping done the hill. When it was about fifty yards away, there was a rush of air from the eagle's beating wings, and Jai saw the bird approaching the hare in a sidelong drive.

'So it hasn't been badly hurt,' thought Jai, feeling a little relieved, for he could not help admiring the great bird. 'Now it has found something else to chase for its dinner.'

The hare saw the eagle and dodged about, making for a clump of junipers. Jai did not know if it was caught or not, because the snow and sleet had increased and both bird and hare were lost in the gathering snowstorm.

The sheep were bleating behind him. One of the lambs looked tired, and he stooped to pick it up. As he did so, he heard a thin, whining sound. It grew louder by the second. Before he could look up, a huge wing caught him across the shoulders and sent him sprawling. The lamb tumbled down the slope with him, into a thorny bilberry bush.

The bush saved them. Jai saw the eagle coming in again, flying low. It was another eagle! One had been vanquished, and now here was another, just as big and fearless, probably the mate of the first eagle.

Jai had lost his stick and there was no way by which he could fight the second eagle. So he crept further into the bush, holding the lamb beneath him. At the same time he began shouting at the top of his voice—both to scare the bird away and to summon help. The eagle could not easily get at them now; but the rest of the flock was exposed on the hillside. Surely the eagle would make for them.

Even as the bird circled and came back in another dive, Jai heard fierce barking. The eagle immediately swung away and rose skywards.

The barking came from Motu. Hearing Jai's shouts and sensing that something was wrong, he had come limping out of the house, ready to do battle. Behind him came another shepherd and—most wonderful of all—Grandmother herself, banging two frying pans together. The barking, the banging and the shouting frightened the eagles away. The sheep scattered too, and it was some time before they could all be rounded up. By then it was snowing heavily.

'Tomorrow we must all go down to Maku,' said the shepherd.

'Yes, it's time we went,' said Grandmother. 'You can read your storybooks again, Jai.'

'I'll have my own story to tell,' said Jai.

When they reached the hut and Jai saw Grandfather, he said, 'Oh, I've forgotten your stick!'

But Motu had picked it up. Carrying it between his teeth, he brought it home and sat down with it in the open doorway. He had decided the cherrywood was good for his teeth and would have chewed it up if Grandmother hadn't taken it from him.

'Never mind,' said Grandfather, sitting up on his cot. 'It isn't the stick that matters. It's the person who holds it.'

THE ELEPHANT AND THE CASSOWARY BIRD

The baby elephant wasn't out of place in our home in north India because India is where elephants belong, and in any case, our house was full of pets brought home by Grandfather, who was in the Forest Service. But the cassowary bird was different. No one had ever seen such a bird before—not in India, that is. Grandfather had picked it up on a voyage to Singapore, where he'd been given the bird by a rubber planter who'd got it from a Dutch trader who'd got it from a man in Indonesia.

Anyway, it ended up at our home in Dehra, and seemed to do quite well in the subtropical climate. It looked like a cross between a turkey and an ostrich, but bigger than the former and smaller than the latter—about five feet in height. It was not a beautiful bird, nor even a friendly one, but it had come to stay, and everyone was curious about it, especially the baby elephant.

Right from the start, the baby elephant took a great interest in the cassowary, a bird unlike any found in the Indian jungles. He would circle round the odd creature, and diffidently examine with his trunk the texture of its stumpy wings. Of course he suspected no evil, and his childlike curiosity encouraged him to take liberties which resulted in an unpleasant experience.

Noticing the baby elephant's attempts to make friends with the rather morose cassowary, we felt a bit apprehensive. Self-contained and sullen, the big bird responded only by slowly and slyly raising one of its powerful legs, in the meantime gazing into space with an innocent air. We knew what the gesture meant; we had seen that treacherous leg raised on many an occasion, and suddenly shooting out with a force that would have done credit to a vicious camel. In fact, camel and cassowary kicks are delivered on the same plan, except that the camel kicks backward like a horse and the bird forward.

We wished to spare our baby elephant a painful experience, and led him away from the bird. But he persisted in his friendly overtures and, one morning, he received an ugly reward. Rapid as lightning, the cassowary hit straight from the hip and knee joints, and the elephant ran squealing to Grandfather.

For several days he avoided the cassowary, and we thought he had learnt his lesson. He crossed and recrossed the compound and the garden, swinging his trunk, thinking furiously. Then, a week later, he appeared on the verandah at breakfast time in his usual cheery, childlike fashion, sidling up to the cassowary as if nothing had happened.

We were struck with amazement at this and so, it seemed, was the bird. Had the painful lesson already been forgotten, and by a member of the elephant tribe noted for its ability to never forget? Another dose of the same medicine would serve the booby right.

The cassowary once more began to draw up its fighting leg with sinister determination. It was nearing the true position for the master kick, kung fu style, when all of a sudden the baby elephant seized with his trunk the cassowary's other leg and pulled it down. There was a clumsy flapping of wings, a tremendous swelling of the bird's wattle, and an undignified getting up, as if it were a floored boxer doing his best to beat the count of ten. The bird then marched off with an attempt to look stately and unconcerned, while we at the breakfast table were convulsed with laughter.

After this, the cassowary bird gave the baby elephant as wide a berth as possible. But they were not forced to coexist for very long. The baby elephant, getting bulky and cumbersome, was sold and now lives in a zoo where he is a favourite with young visitors who love to take rides on his back.

As for the cassowary, he continued to grace our verandah for many years, gaped at but not made much of, while entering on a rather friendless old age.

EXCITING ENCOUNTERS

The following day, Mehmoud was making lamb chops. I liked lamb chops. Mehmoud knew I liked them, and he had an extra chop ready for me, just in case I felt like a pre-lunch snack.

'What was Jim Corbett's favourite dish?' I asked, while dealing with the succulent chop.

'Oh, he liked roast duck. Used to shoot them as they flew up from the jheel.'

'What's a jheel, Mehmoud?'

'A shallow sort of lake. In places you could walk about in the water. Different types of birds would come there in the winter—ducks and geese and all kinds of baglas—herons, you call them. The baglas are not good to eat, but the ducks make a fine roast.

'So we camped beside the jheel and lived on roast duck for a week until everyone was sick of it.'

'Did you go swimming in the jheel?'

'No, it was full of muggers—those long-nosed crocodiles—they'll snap you up if you come within their range! Nasty creatures, those muggermuch. One of them nearly got me.'

'How did that happen, Mehmoud-bhai?'

'Oh, baba, just the memory of it makes me shudder! I'd given everyone their dinner and retired to my tent. It was a hot night and we couldn't sleep. Swarms of mosquitoes rose from the jheel, invaded the tent and attacked me on the face and arms and feet. I dragged my camp cot outside the tent, hoping the breeze would keep the mosquitoes away. After some time they moved on, and I fell asleep, wrapped up in my bedsheet. Towards dawn, I felt my cot quivering, shaking. Was it an earthquake? But no one else was awake. And then the cot started moving! I sat up, looked about me. The cot was moving steadily forward in the direction of the water. And beneath it, holding us up, was a beastly crocodile!

'It gave me the fright of my life, baba. A muggermuch beneath my bed, and I upon it! I cried out for help. Carpet-sahib woke up, rushed out of his tent, his gun in his hands. But it was still dark, and all he could see was my bed moving rapidly towards the jheel.

'Just before we struck the water, I leapt from the cot, and ran up the bank, calling for help. Carpet-sahib saw me then. He ran down the slope, firing at the moving cot. I don't know if he hit the horrible creature, but there was a big splash, and it disappeared into the jheel.'

'And did you recover the cot?'

'No, it floated away and then sank. We did not go after it.'

'And what did Corbett say afterwards?'

'He said I had shown great presence of mind. He said he'd never seen anyone make such a leap for safety!'

'You were a hero, Mehmoud!'

'Thank you, baba. There's time for another lamb chop, if you're hungry.'

'I'm hungry,' I said. 'There's still an hour left to lunchtime. But tell me more about your time with Jim Corbett. Did he like your cooking?'

'Oh, *he* liked it well enough, but his sister was very fussy.'

'He had his sister with him?'

'That's right. He never married, so his sister looked after the household and the shopping and everything connected to the kitchen—except when we were in camp. Then I had a free hand. Carpet-sahib wasn't too fussy about his food, especially when he was out hunting. A sandwich or paratha would keep him going. But if he had guests, he felt he had to give them the best, and then it was hard work for me.

'For instance, there was the Raja of Janakpur, a big, fat man who was very fond of eating—between meals, during meals and after meals. I don't know why he bothered to come on these shikar trips when he could have stayed at home in his palace and feasted day and night. But he needed trophies to hang on the walls of his palace. You were not considered a great king unless your walls were decorated with the stuffed heads of tigers, lions, antelopes, bears—anything that looked dangerous. The Raja could eat and drink all day, but he couldn't go home without a trophy. So he would be hoisted onto an elephant, and sit there in state, firing away at anything that moved in the jungle. He seldom shot anything, but Carpet-sahib would help him out by bringing down a stag or a leopard, and congratulating the Raja on his skill and accuracy.

'They weren't all like that, but some of the Rajas were stupid or even mad. And the Angrej-sahibs—the English—were no better. They, too, had to prove their manliness by shooting a tiger or a leopard. Carpet-sahib was always in demand, because he lived at the edge of the jungle and knew where to look for different animals.

'The Raja of Janakpur was safe on an elephant, but one day he made the mistake of walking into the jungle on foot.

He hadn't gone far when he met a wild boar running at him. A wild boar may not look very dangerous, but it has deadly tusks and is quick to use them. Before the Raja could raise the gun to his shoulder, the pig charged at him. The Raja dropped his gun, turned and ran for his life. But he couldn't run very fast or very far. He tripped and fell, and the boar was almost upon him when I happened along, looking for twigs to make a fire. Luckily, I had a small axe in my hand. I struck the boar over the head. It turned and rammed one of its tusks into my thigh. I struck at it again and again, till it fell dead at my feet. The Raja was nowhere in sight.

'As soon as he got into camp, he sent for his servants and made a hurried departure. Didn't even thank me for saving his life.'

'Were you hurt badly, Mehmoud?'

'I was out of action for a few days. The wound took time to heal. My new masalchi did all the cooking, and the food was so bad that most of the guests left in a hurry. I still have the scar. See, baba!'

Mehmoud drew up his pyjamas and showed me a deep scar on his right thigh.

'You were a hero, Mehmoud,' I said. 'You deserved a reward.'

'My reward is here, baba, preparing these lamb chops for you. Come on, have another. Your parents won't notice if they run short at lunch.'

OWLS IN THE FAMILY

One morning we found a full-fledged baby spotted owlet on the ground by the verandah steps. When Grandfather picked it up, it hissed and clacked its bill, but, after a meal of raw meat and water, settled down for the day under my bed.

The spotted owlet, even when full grown, is only the size of a myna, and has none of the sinister appearance of the larger owls. A pair of them may often be found in an old mango or tamarind tree, and by tapping on the tree trunk you may be able to persuade the bird to show an enquiring face at the entrance to its hole. The bird is not normally afraid of man, nor is it strictly a night-bird; but it prefers to stay at home during the day, as it is sometimes attacked by other birds, who consider all owls as their enemies.

The little owlet was quite happy under my bed. The following day a second owlet was found in almost the same place on the verandah, and only then did we realize that where the rainwater pipe emerged through the roof, there was a rough sort of nest, from which the birds had fallen. We took the second young owl to join the first, and fed them both. When I went to bed they were on the ledge just inside the mosquito netting and, later in the night, their mother found them there. From outside she crooned and gurgled for a long time, and in the morning

I found that she had left a mouse with its tail tucked through the mosquito net! Obviously, she placed no reliance on me as a foster-parent.

The young birds throve and, ten days later at dawn, Grandfather and I took them into the garden to release them. I had placed one on a branch of the mango tree, and was stooping to pick up the other, when I received quite a heavy blow on the back of my head. A second or two later, the mother owl swooped down at Grandfather, but he was agile enough to duck out of its way. Quickly, I placed the second owl under the mango tree. Then, from a safe distance, we watched the mother fly down and lead her offspring into the long grass at the edge of the garden.

We thought she would take her family away from the vicinity of our rather strange household; but next morning, on coming out of my room, I found two young owls standing on the wall just outside the door! I ran to tell Grandfather and, when we came back, we found the mother sitting on the bird-bath ten yards away. She was evidently feeling sorry for her behaviour the previous day, because she greeted us with a soft 'whoo-whoo'.

'Now there's an unselfish mother for you!' said Grandfather. 'It's obvious she'd like them to have a good home. And they're probably getting a bit too big for her to manage.'

So the two owlets became regular members of our household and, strangely enough, were among the few pets that Grandmother took a liking to. She objected to all snakes, most monkeys and some crows, but she took quite a fancy to the owls, and frequently fed them on spaghetti. They seemed quite fond of spaghetti. In fact, the owls became so attached to

Grandmother that they began to show affection towards anyone in a petticoat, including Aunt Mabel, who was terrified of them. She would run shrieking from the room every time one of the birds sidled up to her in a friendly manner.

Forgetful of the fact that Grandfather and I had reared them, the owls would sometimes swell their feathers and snap at anyone in trousers. To avoid displeasing them, Grandfather wore a petticoat at feeding time. This mild form of transvestism appeared to satisfy them. I compromised by wearing an apron.

In response to Grandmother's voice, the owlets would make sounds as gentle and soothing as the purring of a cat; but when wild owls were around, ours would rend the night with blood-curdling shrieks. Their nightly occupation was catching beetles, with which the kitchen-quarters were infested at the time. With their sharp eyes and powerful beaks, they were excellent pest destroyers.

The owls loved to sit and splash in a shallow dish, especially if cold water was poured over them from a jug at the same time. They would get thoroughly wet, jump out on to a perch, shake themselves, then return for a second splash and sometimes a third. During the day they dozed in large cages under the trees in the garden. They needed cages for protection against attacks from wild birds. At night they had the freedom of the house, where they exercised their wings as much as they liked. Superstitious folk, who dread the cry of the owl, may be interested to know that—mice excepted—there were no untoward deaths in the house during the owls' residence.

Looking back on those owlish days, I carry in my mind a picture of Grandmother with a contented look in her rocking-chair. Once, on entering her room while she was having an afternoon nap, I saw that one of the owls had crawled up her pillow till its head was snuggled under her ear. Both Grandmother and the little owl were snoring.

THOSE THREE BEARS

Most Himalayan villages lie in the valleys, where there are small streams, some farmland and protection from the biting winds that come through the mountain passes in winter. The houses are usually made of large stones and have sloping slate roofs so the heavy monsoon rain can run off easily. During the sunny autumn months, the roofs are often covered with pumpkins, left there to ripen in the sun.

One October night, when I was sleeping at a friend's house in a village in these hills, I was awakened by a rumbling and thumping on the roof. I woke my friend and asked him what was happening.

'It's only a bear,' he said.

'Is it trying to get in?'

'No. It's after the pumpkins.'

A little later, when we looked out of a window, we saw a black bear making off through a field, leaving a trail of half-eaten pumpkins.

In winter, when snow covers the higher ranges, the Himalayan bears come to lower altitudes in search of food. Sometimes they forage in fields and because they are shortsighted and suspicious of anything that moves, they can be dangerous. But, like most wild animals, they avoid humans as much as possible.

Village folk always advise me to run downhill if chased by a bear. They say bears find it easier to run uphill than down. I am yet to be chased by a bear, and will happily skip the experience. But I have seen a few of these mountain bears in India, and they are always fascinating to watch.

Himalayan bears enjoy pumpkins, corn, plums and apricots. Once, while I was sitting in an oak tree hoping to see a pair of pine martens that lived nearby, I heard the whining grumble of a bear, and presently a small bear ambled into the clearing beneath the tree.

He was little more than a cub, and I was not alarmed. I sat very still, waiting to see what he would do.

He put his nose to the ground and sniffed his way along until he came to a large anthill. Here he began huffing and puffing, blowing rapidly in and out of his nostrils, so that the dust from the anthill flew in all directions. But the anthill had been deserted and so, grumbling, the bear made his way up a nearby plum tree. Soon he was perched high in the branches. It was then that he saw me.

The bear at once scrambled several feet higher up the tree and lay flat on a branch. Since it wasn't a very big branch, there was a lot of bear showing on either side. He tucked his head behind another branch. He could no longer see me, so he apparently was satisfied that he was hidden, although he couldn't help grumbling.

Like all bears, this one was full of curiosity. So, slowly, inch by inch, his black snout appeared over the edge of the branch. As soon as he saw me, he drew his head back and hid his face.

He did this several times. I waited until he wasn't looking, then moved some way down my tree. When the bear looked over and saw that I was missing, he was so pleased that he stretched right across to another branch and helped himself to a plum. I couldn't help bursting into laughter.

The startled young bear tumbled out of the tree, dropped through the branches some fifteen feet, and landed with a thump in a pile of dried leaves. He was unhurt, but fled from the clearing, grunting and squealing all the way.

Another time, my friend Prem told me, a bear had been active in his cornfield. We took up a post at night in an old cattle shed, which gave a clear view of the moonlit field.

A little after midnight, a female bear came down to the edge of the field. She seemed to sense that we had been about. She was hungry, however. So, after standing on her hind legs and peering around to make sure the field was empty, she came cautiously out of the forest.

Her attention was soon distracted by some Tibetan prayer flags, which had been strung between two trees. She gave a grunt of disapproval and began to back away, but the fluttering of the flags was a puzzle that she wanted to solve. So she stopped and watched them.

Soon the bear advanced to within a few feet of the flags, examining them from various angles. Then, seeing that they posed no danger, she went right up to the flags and pulled them down. Grunting with apparent satisfaction, she moved into the field of corn.

Prem had decided that he didn't want to lose any more of his crop, so he started shouting. His children woke up and soon came running from the house, banging on empty kerosene tins.

Deprived of her dinner, the bear made off in a bad temper. She ran downhill at a good speed, and I was glad that I was not in her way.

Uphill or downhill, an angry bear is best given a very wide path.

THE HARE IN THE MOON

A long time ago, when animals could talk, there lived in a forest four wise creatures—a hare, a jackal, an otter and a monkey.

They were good friends, and every evening they would sit together in a forest glade to discuss the events of the day, exchange advice and make good resolutions. The hare was the noblest and wisest of the four. He believed in the superiority of men and women, and was always telling his friends tales of human goodness and wisdom.

One evening, when the moon rose in the sky—and in those days the moon's face was clear and unmarked—the hare looked up at it carefully and said: 'Tomorrow good men will observe a fast, for I can see that it will be the middle of the month. They will eat no food before sunset, and during the day they will give alms to any beggar or holy man who may meet them. Let us promise to do the same. In that way, we can come a little closer to human beings in dignity and wisdom.'

The others agreed, and then went their different ways.

Next day, the otter got up, stretched himself and was preparing to get his breakfast when he remembered the vow he had taken with his friends.

'If I keep my word, how hungry I shall be by evening!' he

thought. 'I'd better make sure that there's plenty to eat once the fast is over.' He set off towards the river.

A fisherman had caught several large fish early that morning, and had buried them in the sand, planning to return for them later. The otter soon smelt them out.

'A supper all ready for me!' he said to himself. 'But since it's a holy day, I mustn't steal.' Instead he called out: 'Does anyone own this fish?'

There being no answer, the otter carried the fish off to his home, setting it aside for his evening meal. Then he locked his front door and slept all through the day, undisturbed by beggars or holy men asking for alms.

Both the monkey and the jackal felt much the same way when they got up that morning. They remembered their vows but thought it best to have something put by for the evening. The jackal found some stale meat in someone's back yard. 'Ah, that should improve with age,' he thought, and took it home for his evening meal. And the monkey climbed a mango tree and picked a bunch of mangoes. Like the otter, they decided to sleep through the day.

The hare woke early. Shaking his long ears, he came out of his burrow and sniffed the dew-drenched grass.

'When evening comes, I can have my fill of grass,' he thought. 'But if a beggar or holy man comes my way, what can I give him? I cannot offer him grass, and I have nothing else to give. I shall have to offer myself. Most men seem to relish the flesh of the hare. We're good to eat, I'm told.' And pleased with this solution to the problem, he scampered off.

Now God Sakka had been resting on a cloud not far away, and he had heard the hare speaking aloud.

'I will test him,' said the god. 'Surely no hare can be so noble and unselfish.'

Towards evening, God Sakka descended from his cloud, and assuming the form of an old priest, he sat down near the hare's burrow. When the animal came home from his romp, he said: 'Good evening, little hare. Can you give me something to eat? I have been fasting all day, and am so hungry that I cannot pray.'

The hare, remembering his vow, said: 'Is it true that men enjoy eating the flesh of the hare?'

'Quite true,' said the priest.

'In that case,' said the hare, 'since I have no other food to offer you, you can make a meal of me.'

'But I am a holy man, and this is a holy day, and I may not kill any living creature with my own hands.'

'Then collect some dry sticks and set them alight. I will leap into the flames myself, and when I am roasted you can eat me.'

God Sakka marvelled at these words, but he was still not quite convinced, so he caused a fire to spring up from the earth. The hare, without any hesitation, jumped into the flames.

'What's happening?' called the hare after a while. 'The fire surrounds me, but not a hair of my coat is singed. In fact, I'm feeling quite cold!'

As the hare spoke, the fire died down, and he found himself sitting on the cool sweet grass. Instead of the old priest, there stood before him God Sakka in all his radiance.

'I am God Sakka, little hare, and having heard your vow, I wanted to test your sincerity. Such unselfishness of yours deserves immortality. It must be known throughout the world.'

God Sakka then stretched out his hand towards the mountain, and drew from it some of the essence which ran in its veins. This he threw towards the moon, which had just risen, and instantly the outline of the hare appeared on the moon's surface.

Then leaving the hare in a bed of sweet grass, he said: 'For ever and ever, little hare, you shall look down from the moon upon the world, to remind men of the old truth, "Give to others, and the gods will give to you."'

THE WHITE ELEPHANT

Long ago, when animals could talk like humans, a great herd of elephants lived in a forest near the Himalaya mountains. The finest elephant in the tribe was a rare white animal.

Unfortunately the mother of this elephant was old and blind and although her son gathered sweet wild fruits for her every day, he was often angry to find the other elephants had stolen his mother's food.

'Mother,' he said, 'it would be better if you and I were to go and live alone in a distant cave I have discovered.'

The mother elephant agreed and for a time the two of them lived happily in a peaceful spot near a glade of wild fruit trees. Until one evening they heard loud cries coming from the great forest.

'That is the voice of a man in distress,' said the white elephant. 'I must go and see if I can help him.'

'Do not go, my son,' said his mother. 'I am old and blind but I know the ways of human beings towards us. Your goodness will be rewarded by treachery.'

But the white elephant could not bear to think of anyone in trouble and he hurried down to the lake in the direction of the cries, where he discovered a man who was a forester.

'Don't fear me, stranger,' he said. 'Tell me how I can help you.'

The forester told the white elephant he had been lost for seven days and nights and could not find his way back to Benares where he lived.

'Climb on my back,' said the elephant cheerfully, 'and I will carry you home.'

The elephant carried the man swiftly through the forest until they reached open country; then he left him on the outskirts of the city before returning to his cave.

Now the forester was a greedy and cunning man and he knew that before he left Benares, the king's favourite elephant had died. 'The king would reward me richly,' thought the man, 'if I captured this fine animal for him,' and straightaway he asked for a royal audience.

The king was delighted with the description of the white elephant. 'I would love to possess such a fine creature. Go back to the forest with a band of my most skilful trainers and if they succeed in capturing this rare elephant, you shall be well rewarded.'

The forester had cunningly noted landmarks while riding back to Benares and he led the trainers to the lake where the white elephant was gathering bamboo stems for his mother's evening meal. When the elephant saw the forester with the band of trainers, he knew he had been betrayed.

He tried to escape but the trainers pursued him and soon succeeded in capturing him. Then they led him through the forest and entered Benares in triumph.

The poor mother elephant, waiting for her son to return, felt certain that he had been captured.

'What shall I do without him?' she cried. 'Who will bring me food and lead me to the lotus lake for water.'

The heart of her son was equally heavy. 'What will she do

without me,' he thought, 'if only I had listened to her advice.'

In spite of his unhappy look, the elephant found favour with the king, who declared he would ride no other animal. The elephant's stable was richly decorated in his honour and the king rode him in state through the city.

But a few days later the trainers came to the king in great distress saying, 'Your Majesty, the white elephant is very sick and will eat nothing.'

The king hurried to the stable and when he saw the elephant's look of despair, he said, 'Good animal, how you have changed! Why do you refuse to eat? Anything you wish will be granted to you.'

'Great King,' answered the elephant mournfully, 'all I desire is to return to my poor blind mother in the forest, for while she is alone and starving, how can I eat?'

Now the king was a good king and although he badly wanted the elephant for himself, he said at once, 'Noble animal, your goodness puts mankind to shame. I give you your freedom to return to your mother at once.'

The elephant thanked the king with a loud trumpeting, and left the city and went crashing back through the forest. When he reached the cave, he found to his joy that his mother was still alive.

'Ah, my son,' she said when he told her his story. 'You should have listened to me. Human beings have always brought harm to our race.'

'Not all of them, mother,' he said triumphantly. 'The king is noble and generous or I should still be in captivity. Let's forget the treachery of the forester and think only of the king's goodness!'

THE BOY WHO COULD SEE FOOTSTEPS

About fifty miles from the city of Benares, in India, there once lived, in a great dark cave, a creature called a Yakka. She had the face of a horse and the body of a woman. She was strong and fierce as a tigress. And she lived upon the flesh of any man or beast whom she could trap.

One day the Yakka caught a school teacher who was travelling alone towards Benares. She carried him off with great swiftness into her cave. When she saw that he was young and handsome, she asked him whether, if she spared his life, he would marry her. And the teacher, thinking that of two evils this would be the lesser, agreed to become her husband.

Afterwards, the Yakka grew more and more humane and gentle, gave up eating people and tried in various ways to improve her mind. However, she always feared that her teacher-husband would run away if he could, so she used to roll a huge stone in front of the entrance to the cave whenever she went out to collect food. And in this way the poor teacher was kept a prisoner.

The Yakka was happy enough, and spent her days lying in wait for passing caravans. Fearful travellers were only too ready to part with food and spices, and upon these the Yakka and her husband lived. At length a little son was born to them. In spite of being cooped up in a dark, cold cave, he grew into a strong and clever boy. The Yakka was devoted to him and did all she could to make him and his father comfortable and happy. But the poor teacher pined for freedom. He longed for sunshine and fresh breezes, for the sights and sounds of the city.

One day his son said to him, 'Father, why is my mother's face so different from ours?'

'Because she is a Yakka, son, and we are men.'

'Then why do we live with her in this gloomy cave, instead of among our fellows?'

'Because of the great stone which the Yakka rolls in front of the cave's entrance. It is too heavy for me to move. But you have your mother's strength—see if you can move it.'

The boy sprang up and, setting his shoulder to the stone, easily rolled it aside. He seized his father by the hand and they ran until the teacher, unused to the light and air, became half-blind and dizzy from the exertion. Even the boy was breathless. They sat down to rest; but, before they had recovered enough to go on, they heard the thud of the Yakka's feet in pursuit, and she soon caught up with them.

'Oh, thankless husband and more thankless child!' she cried. 'Why do you run away? What did you lack in my home? You lay upon beds of leaf and moss. You ate dates and drank the wine of pomegranates.'

'But, Mother,' answered the boy, 'we lack air and light, and these are more necessary to us than wine and dates.'

'Come back with me and you shall have both,' she said. So they returned, and she broke the great stone into splinters, and allowed them to wander into the woods and up and down the road; but whenever they got more than a kilometre away from the cave they would always hear her great feet thudding after them.

One day the boy found out that his mother's power extended only as far as the river one way, and as far as the mountains the other way. So when she was fast asleep, on a dark night, he and his father crept out of the cave and fled towards the river. They had just managed to reach the bank when they heard the sound of the Yakka's feet thudding after them. But the boy did not pause. He hoisted his father on his back and waded up to his waist in the stream. Then, safe from the Yakka's power, he looked back. 'Come back, come back!' she cried.

'I will return one day,' replied the boy. 'We are men, and it is right that we should dwell among men. But you are my mother and have given me your love. I will return.'

The Yakka knelt upon the river bank and wept tears into the running water; but father and son had already made their way to the other bank. She no longer pleaded with them; but, because she loved her child dearly, she told him he should take from her a talisman that should prove of great value to him in the world of men.

'Take this stone,' she said, throwing it across to him, 'and hang it about your neck. By its power you will be able to see footsteps even twelve years after they have been made upon the ground by the feet of men.'

The boy caught the stone and fastened it round his neck. Then, waving goodbye, he and his father took the road to Benares. All the way the boy saw thousands of footprints—prints that had long since disappeared from the sight of ordinary humans—and at first he was confused by these tell-tale signs of the men and women who had come and gone that way over the years; but he soon got used to them, and even began to single out the more interesting footprints, and by the time they reached Benares, he had come to the conclusion that no two footprints were the same.

As soon as they arrived in the city, they went straight to the king's palace, where the boy's father was appointed a teacher in a school for young princes. The king soon heard from his ministers that the teacher's son had the power of seeing long-vanished footsteps.

'Should any robber tamper with the king's treasury, my son can trace the thief and find the valuables,' the teacher announced to the chief minister. 'Why not ask your royal master to take the boy into his service?'

The king was only too glad to do so, for he was extremely rich and miserly, and lived in daily and nightly fear of being robbed.

'How much does this boy expect us to pay him?' was his first question.

'A thousand rupees daily,' said the minister.

'Too much, too much!' complained the king. But the boy held out for that sum, and the king at last agreed to it.

Some months passed and, as the fame of the boy's gift passed through Benares, no attempts were made to rob the treasury.

The king was still unhappy about the fee he was paying the boy. 'How are we to know that he is not an impostor?' he complained. 'We are paying him a thousand rupees daily, and he does nothing but sit upon an expensive rug near my marble fountain, playing chess with his father and drinking lemonade! I'm being cheated!'

The next night two thieves broke into the vaults where the

treasure was kept. They took many jewels and much money, which they placed in sacks. Then they walked three times round the palace, passed through the gardens, climbed the wall by means of a ladder and finally reached a tank in the middle of a meadow. They dropped the sacks into the tank and then disappeared into the night.

Next day, the king raised a terrible outcry. Some of the most precious of the crown jewels had been stolen! The thief must be found! Where was the boy who could see footsteps?

'Here I am, sire,' said the boy, hurrying to the king's audience chamber. 'I shall trace the thieves at once!'

And starting from the vaults, he walked three times round the palace, passed through the gardens, climbed the wall at a certain spot and finally reached the tank in the meadow. He ordered a diver to enter the water and bring up whatever he could find at the bottom.

'I have seen the footsteps of two men all the way,' he said, 'and they are men of distinction.'

For some moments there was deep silence as they all stood around gazing down into the tank.

People clapped and cheered as the diver brought up, one by one, the bags full of treasure. But the king, who appeared disappointed to see how well the boy was earning his salary, whispered to his minister, 'This is all very well. He has recovered the treasure. But can he trace the thieves? Let us test him further.' And turning to the boy, he said aloud, 'Now find me these thieves.'

'That should not be necessary now that the jewels and money are recovered,' said the boy thoughtfully.

But the king insisted. 'I shall cut your salary by half if you cannot find the thieves. My heart longs to punish those rascals.'

'Be careful of what you say, sire,' said the boy. 'If it is someone upon whom the people depend, what shall the people do?'

'Punish him, of course!' said the king, laughing.

'Shall I name the thieves, then?' asked the boy for the last time.

'Yes, or I cut your thousand rupees daily down to a hundred!'

'Yourself and your minister, O King! You are the thieves!'

And when the people learned that their rulers stooped to all this trickery to fill their private coffers with wealth that should have been used for the benefit of the kingdom, they decided that these two were not worthy to hold positions of trust over them. So they dethroned the king and exiled him and his minister, and gave the crown to the boy who saw their footsteps.

And did the boy ever see his mother, the Yakka, again?

No one knew for certain, but it was said that he would mysteriously disappear on full-moon nights. And although his ministers followed him to try and find out where he went, they never succeeded, because the boy was careful not to leave any footprints of his own.

THE PARROT WHO WOULDN'T TALK

'You're no beauty! Can't talk, can't sing, can't dance!'

With these words Aunt Ruby would taunt the unfortunate parakeet who glared morosely at everyone from his ornamental cage at one end of the long veranda of Granny's bungalow in north India.

In those distant days, almost everyone—Indian or European—kept a pet parrot or parakeet, or 'lovebird' as some of the smaller ones were called. Sometimes these birds became great talkers, or rather mimics, and would learn to recite entire mantras (religious chants), or admonitions to the children of the house, such as *'Paro, beta, paro!'* ('Study, child, study!') or, for the benefit of boys like me—'Don't be greedy, don't be greedy.'

These expressions were, of course, picked up by the parrot over a period of time, after many repetitions by whichever member of the household had taken on the task of teaching the bird to talk.

But our parrot refused to talk.

He'd been bought by Aunt Ruby from a birdcatcher who'd visited all the houses on our road, selling caged birds ranging from colourful budgerigars to chirpy little munnias and even common sparrows that had been dabbed with paint and passed off as some exotic species. Neither Granny nor Grandfather were keen on keeping caged birds as pets, but Aunt Ruby threatened to throw a tantrum if she did not get her way—and Aunt Ruby's tantrums were dreadful to behold.

Anyway, she insisted on keeping the parrot and teaching him to talk. But the bird took an instant dislike to my aunt and resisted all her blandishments.

'Kiss, kiss,' Aunt Ruby would coo, putting her face close to the barge of the cage. But the parrot would back away, his beady little eyes getting even smaller with anger at the prospect of being kissed by Aunt Ruby. And, on one occasion, he lunged forward without warning and knocked my aunt's spectacles off her nose.

After that, Aunt Ruby gave up her endearments and became quite hostile towards the poor bird, making faces at him and calling out, 'Can't talk, can't sing, can't dance!' and other nasty comments.

It fell upon me, then ten years old, to feed the parrot, and he seemed quite happy to receive green chillies and ripe tomatoes from my hands, these delicacies being supplemented by slices of mango, for it was then the mango season. It also gave me an opportunity to consume a couple of mangoes while feeding the parrot.

One afternoon, while everyone was indoors enjoying a siesta, I gave the parrot his lunch and then deliberately left the cage door open. Seconds later, the bird was winging his way to the freedom of the mango orchard.

At the same time Grandfather came on to the veranda, and remarked, 'I see your aunt's parrot has escaped.'

'The door was quite loose,' I said with a shrug. 'Well, I don't suppose we'll see it again.'

Aunt Ruby was upset at first, and threatened to buy another bird. We put her off by promising to buy her a bowl of goldfish.

'But goldfish don't talk,' she protested.

'Well, neither did your bird,' said Grandfather. 'So we'll get you a gramophone. You can listen to Clara Cluck all day. They say she sings like a nightingale.'

I thought we'd never see the parrot again, but he probably missed his green chillies, because a few days later, I found the bird sitting on the veranda railing, looking expectantly at me with his head cocked to one side. Unselfishly, I gave the parrot half of my mango.

While the bird was enjoying the mango, Aunt Ruby emerged from her room and, with a cry of surprise, called out, 'Look, my parrot's come back! He must have missed me!'

With a loud squawk, the parrot flew out of her reach and, perching on the nearest rose bush, glared at Aunt Ruby and shrieked at her in my aunt's familiar tones, 'You're no beauty! Can't talk, can't sing, can't dance!'

Aunt Ruby went ruby red and dashed indoors. But that wasn't the end of the affair. The parrot became a frequent visitor to the garden and veranda and whenever he saw Aunt Ruby he would call out, 'You're no beauty, you're no beauty! Can't sing, can't dance!'

The parrot had learnt to talk after all.

THE TIGER KING'S GIFT

Long ago, in the days of the ancient Pandya kings of south India, a father and his two sons lived in a village near Madura. The father was an astrologer, but he had never become famous, and so was very poor. The elder son was called Chellan; the younger Gangan. When the time came for the father to put off his earthly body, he gave his few fields to Chellan, and a palm leaf with some words scratched on it to Gangan.

These were the words that Gangan read:

'From birth, poverty;
For ten years, captivity;
On the seashore, death.
For a little while happiness shall follow.'

'This must be my fortune,' said Gangan to himself, 'and it doesn't seem to be much of a fortune. I must have done something terrible in a former birth. But I will go as a pilgrim to Papanasam and do penance. If I can expiate my sin, I may have better luck.'

His only possession was a water jar of hammered copper, which had belonged to his grandfather. He coiled a rope round the jar, in case he needed to draw water from a well. Then he put a little rice into a bundle, said farewell to his brother, and set out.

As he journeyed, he had to pass through a great forest. Soon he had eaten all his food and drunk all the water in his jar. In the heat of the day he became very thirsty.

At last he came to an old, disused well. As he looked down into it, he could see that a winding stairway had once gone round it down to the water's edge, and that there had been four landing places at different heights down this stairway, so that those who wanted to fetch water might descend the stairway to the level of the water and fill their water pots with ease, regardless of whether the well was full, or three-quarters full, or half full or only one-quarter full.

Now the well was nearly empty. The stairway had fallen away. Gangan could not go down to fill his water jar so he uncoiled his rope, tied his jar to it and slowly let it down. To his amazement, as it was going down past the first landing place, a huge striped paw shot out and caught it, and a growling voice called out: 'Oh Lord of Charity, have mercy! The stair is fallen. I die unless you save me! Fear me not. Though King of Tigers, I will not harm you.'

Gangan was terrified at hearing a tiger speak, but his kindness overcame his fear, and with a great effort, he pulled the beast up.

The Tiger King—for it was indeed the Lord of All Tigers—bowed his head before Gangan, and reverently paced around him thrice from right to left as worshippers do round a shrine.

'Three days ago,' said the Tiger King, 'a goldsmith passed by, and I followed him. In terror he jumped down this well and fell on the fourth landing place below. He is there still. When I leaped after him I fell on the first landing place. On the third landing is a rat who jumped in when a great snake chased him. And on the second landing, above the rat, is the snake who followed him. They will all clamour for you to draw them up.

'Free the snake, by all means. He will be grateful and will not harm you. Free the rat, if you will. But do not free the goldsmith, for he cannot be trusted. Should you free him, you will surely repent of your kindness. He will do you an injury for his own profit. But remember that I will help you whenever you need me.'

Then the Tiger King bounded away into the forest.

Gangan had forgotten his thirst while he stood before the Tiger King. Now he felt it more than before, and again let down his water jar.

As it passed the second landing place on the ruined staircase, a huge snake darted out and twisted itself round the rope. 'Oh, Incarnation of Mercy, save me!' it hissed. 'Unless you help me, I must die here, for I cannot climb the sides of the well. Help me, and I will always serve you!'

Gangan's heart was again touched, and he drew up the snake. It glided round him as if he were a holy being. 'I am the Serpent King,' it said. 'I was chasing a rat. It jumped into the well and fell on the third landing below. I followed, but fell on the second landing. Then the goldsmith leaped in and fell on the fourth landing place, while the tiger fell on the top landing. You saved the Tiger King. You have saved me. You may save the rat, if you wish. But do not free the goldsmith. He is not to be trusted. He will harm you if you help him. But I will not forget you, and will come to your aid if you call upon me.'

Then the King of Snakes disappeared into the long grass of the forest.

Gangan let down his jar once more, eager to quench his thirst. But as the jar passed the third landing, the rat leaped into it.

'After the Tiger King, what is a rat?' said Gangan to himself, and pulled the jar up.

Like the tiger and the snake, the rat did reverence, and offered his services if ever they were needed. And like the tiger and the snake, he warned Gangan against the goldsmith. Then the Rat King—for he was none other—ran off into a hole among the roots of a banyan tree.

By this time, Gangan's thirst was becoming unbearable. He almost flung the water jar down the well. But again the rope was seized, and Gangan heard the goldsmith beg piteously to be hauled up.

'Unless I pull him out of the well, I shall never get any water,' groaned Gangan. 'And after all, why not help the unfortunate man?' So with a great struggle—for he was a very fat goldsmith—Gangan got him out of the well and on to the grass beside him.

The goldsmith had much to say. But before listening to him, Gangan let his jar down into the well a fifth time. And then he drank till he was satisfied.

'Friend and deliverer!' cried the goldsmith. 'Don't believe what those beasts have said about me! I live in the holy city of Tenkasi, only a day's journey north of Papanasam. Come and visit me whenever you are there. I will show you that I am not an ungrateful man.' And he took leave of Gangan and went his way.

'From birth, poverty.'

Gangan resumed his pilgrimage, begging his way to Papanasam.

There he stayed many weeks, performing all the ceremonies which pilgrims should perform, bathing at the waterfall, and watching the Brahmin priests feeding the fishes in the sacred stream. He visited other shrines, going as far as Cape Comorin, the southernmost tip of India, where he bathed in the sea. Then he came back through the jungles of Travancore.

He had started on his pilgrimage with his copper water jar and nothing more. After months of wanderings, it was still the only thing he owned. The first prophecy on the palm leaf had already come true: '*From birth, poverty*.'

During his wanderings Gangan had never once thought of the Tiger King and the others, but as he walked wearily along in his rags, he saw a ruined well by the roadside, and it reminded him of his wonderful adventure. And just to see if the Tiger King was genuine, he called out: 'Oh King of Tigers, let me see you!'

No sooner had he spoken than the Tiger King leaped out of the bushes, carrying in his mouth a glittering golden helmet, embedded with precious stones.

It was the helmet of King Pandya, the monarch of the land.

The king had been waylaid and killed by robbers, for the sake of the jewelled helmet; but they in turn had fallen prey to the tiger, who had walked away with the helmet.

Gangan, of course, knew nothing about all this, and when the Tiger King laid the helmet at his feet, he stood stupefied at its splendour and his own good luck.

After the Tiger King had left him, Gangan thought of the goldsmith. 'He will take the jewels out of the helmet, and I will sell some of them. Others I will take home.' So he wrapped the helmet in a rag and made his way to Tenkasi.

In the Tenkasi bazaar he soon found the goldsmith's shop. When they had talked a while, Gangan uncovered the golden helmet. The goldsmith—who knew its worth far better than Gangan—gloated over it, and at once agreed to take out the jewels and sell a few so that Gangan might have some money to spend.

'Now let me examine this helmet at leisure,' said the goldsmith. 'You go to the shrines, worship, and come back. I will then tell you what your treasure is worth.'

Gangan went off to worship at the famous shrines of Tenkasi. And as soon as he had gone, the goldsmith went off to the local magistrate.

'Did not the herald of King Pandya's son come here only yesterday and announce that he would give half his kingdom to anyone who discovered his father's murderer?' he asked. 'Well, I have found the killer. He has brought the king's jewelled helmet to me this very day.'

The magistrate called his guards, and they all hurried to the goldsmith's shop and reached it just as Gangan returned from his tour of the temples.

'Here is the helmet!' exclaimed the goldsmith to the magistrate. 'And here is the villain who murdered the king to get it!'

The guards seized poor Gangan and marched him off to Madura, the capital of the Pandya kingdom, and brought him before the murdered king's son. When Gangan tried to explain about the Tiger King, the goldsmith called him a liar, and the new king had him thrown into the death cell, a deep, well-like pit, dug into the ground in a courtyard of the palace. The only entrance to it was a hole in the pavement of the courtyard. Here Gangan was left to die of hunger and thirst.

At first Gangan lay helpless where he had fallen. Then,

looking around him, he found himself on a heap of bones, the bones of those who before him had died in the dungeon; and he was watched by an army of rats who were waiting to gnaw his dead body. He remembered how the Tiger King had warned him against the goldsmith, and had promised help if ever it was needed.

'I need help now,' groaned Gangan, and shouted for the Tiger King, the Snake King, and the Rat King.

For some time nothing happened. Then all the rats in the dungeon suddenly left him and began burrowing in a corner between some of the stones in the wall. Presently, Gangan saw that the hole was quite large, and that many other rats were coming and going, working at the same tunnel. And then the Rat King himself came through the little passage, and he was followed by the Snake King, while a great roar from outside told Gangan that the Tiger King was there.

'We cannot get you out of this place,' said the Snake King. 'The walls are too strong. But the armies of the Rat King will bring rice cakes from the palace kitchens, and sweets from the shops in the bazaars, and rags soaked in water. They will not let you die. And from this day on the tigers and the snakes will slay tenfold, and the rats will destroy grain and cloth as never before. Before long the people will begin to complain. Then, when you hear anyone passing in front of your cell, shout: "These disasters are the results of your ruler's injustice! But I can save you from them!" At first they will pay no attention. But after some time they will take you out, and at your word we will stop the sacking and the slaughter. And then they will honour you.'

'For ten years, captivity.'

For ten years the tigers killed. The serpents struck. The rats destroyed. And at last the people wailed, 'The gods are plaguing us.'

All the while, Gangan cried out to those who came near his cell, declaring that he could save them; they thought he was a madman. So ten years passed, and the second prophecy on the palm leaf was fulfilled.

At last, the Snake King made his way into the palace and bit the king's only daughter. She was dead in a few minutes.

The king called for all the snake charmers and offered half his kingdom to any one of them who would restore his daughter to life. None of them was able to do so. Then the king's servants remembered the cries of Gangan and remarked that there was a madman in the dungeons who kept insisting that he could bring an end to all their troubles. The king at once ordered the dungeon to be opened. Ladders were let down. Men descended and found Gangan, looking more like a ghost than a man. His hair had grown so long that none could see his face. The king did not remember him, but Gangan soon reminded the king of how he had condemned him without enquiry, on the word of the goldsmith.

The king grovelled in the dust before Gangan, begged forgiveness, and entreated him to restore the dead princess to life.

'Bring me the body of the princess,' said Gangan.

Then he called on the Tiger King and the Snake King to come and give life to the princess. As soon as they entered the royal chamber, the princess was restored to life.

Glad as they were to see the princess alive, the king and his courtiers were filled with fear at the sight of the Tiger King and the Snake King. But the tiger and the snake hurt no one, and at a second prayer from Gangan, they brought life to all those they had slain.

And when Gangan made a third petition, the Tiger, the Snake and the Rat Kings ordered their subjects to stop pillaging the Pandya kingdom, so long as the king did no further injustice.

'Let us find that treacherous goldsmith and put him in the dungeon,' said the Tiger King.

But Gangan wanted no vengeance. That very day he set out for his village to see his brother, Chellan, once more. But when he left the Pandya king's capital, he took the wrong road. After much wandering, he found himself on the seashore.

Now it happened that his brother was also making a journey in those parts, and it was their fate that they should meet by the sea. When Gangan saw his brother, his gladness was so sudden and so great that he fell down dead.

And so the third prophecy was fulfilled:

'On the seashore, death.'

Chellan, as he came along the shore road, had seen a half-ruined shrine of Pillaiyar, the elephant-headed god of good luck. Chellan was a very devout servant of Pillaiyar, and, the day being a festival day, he felt it was his duty to worship the god. But it was also his duty to perform the funeral rites for his brother.

The seashore was lonely. There was no one to help him. It would take hours to collect fuel and driftwood enough for a funeral pyre. For a while Chellan did not know what to do. But at last he took up the body and carried it to Pillaiyar's temple.

Then he addressed the god. 'This is my brother's body,' he said. 'I am unclean because I have touched it. I must go and bathe in the sea. Then I will come and worship you, and afterwards I will burn my brother's body. Meanwhile, I leave it in your care.'

Chellan left, and the god told his attendant *ganas* (goblins) to watch over the body. These *ganas* are inclined to be mischievous, and when the god wasn't looking, they gobbled up the body of Gangan.

When Chellan came back from bathing, he reverently worshipped Pillaiyar. He then looked for his brother's body. It was not to be found. Anxiously he demanded it of the god. Pillaiyar called on his goblins to produce it. Terrified, they confessed to what they had done.

Chellan reproached the god for the misdeeds of his attendants. And Pillaiyar felt so much pity for him that by his divine power he restored dead Gangan's body to Chellan, and brought Gangan to life again.

The two brothers then returned to King Pandya's capital, where Gangan married the princess and became king when her father died.

And so the fourth prophecy was fulfilled:

'For a little while happiness shall follow.'

But there are wise men who say that the lines of the prophecy were wrongly read and understood, and that the whole should run:

'From birth, poverty;
For ten years, captivity;
On the seashore, death for a little while;
Happiness shall follow.'

It is the last two lines that are different. And this must be the correct version, because when happiness came to Gangan it was not 'for a little while'. When the goddess of good fortune did arrive, she stayed in his palace for many, many years.

COPPERFIELD IN THE JUNGLE

Grandfather never hunted wild animals; he could not understand the pleasure some people obtained from killing the creatures of our forests. Birds and animals, he felt, had as much right to live as humans. There was some justification in killing for food—most animals did—but none at all in killing just for the fun of it.

At the age of twelve, I did not have the same high principles as Grandfather. Nevertheless, I disliked anything to do with shikar or hunting. I found it terribly boring.

Uncle Henry and some of his sporting friends once took me on a shikar expedition into the Terai forests of the Siwaliks. The prospect of a whole week in the jungle as camp follower to several adults with guns filled me with dismay. I knew that long, weary hours would be spent tramping behind these tall, professional-looking huntsmen. They could only speak in terms of bagging this tiger or that wild elephant, when all they ever got, if they were lucky, was a wild hare or a partridge. Tigers and excitement, it seemed, came only to Jim Corbett.

This particular expedition proved to be different from others. There were four men with guns, and at the end of the week, all that they had shot were two miserable, underweight wild fowls. But I managed, on our second day in the jungle, to be left behind at the rest house. And, in the course of a morning's exploration of the old bungalow, I discovered a shelf of books half-hidden in a corner of the back veranda.

Who had left them there? A literary forest officer? A memsahib who had been bored by her husband's camp-fire boasting? Or someone who had no interest in the 'manly' sport of slaughtering wild animals and had brought his library along to pass the time?

Or possibly the poor fellow had gone into the jungle one day, as a gesture towards his more bloodthirsty companions, and been trampled by an elephant, or gored by a wild boar, or (more likely) accidentally shot by one of the shikaris and his sorrowing friends had taken his remains away and left his books behind.

Anyway, there they were—a shelf of some thirty volumes, obviously untouched for many years. I wiped the thick dust off the covers and examined the titles. As my reading tastes had not yet formed, I was willing to try anything. The bookshelf was varied in its contents—and my own interests have since remained fairly universal.

On that fateful day in the forest rest house, I discovered P.G. Wodehouse and read his *Love among the Chickens,* an early Ukridge story and still one of my favourites. By the time the perspiring hunters came home late in the evening, with their spent cartridges and lame excuses, I had made a start with M.R. James's *Ghost Stories of an Antiquary,* which had me hooked on ghost stories for the rest of my life. It kept me awake most of the night, until the oil in the kerosene lamp had finished.

Next morning, fresh and optimistic again, the shikaris set out for a different area, where they hoped to 'bag a tiger'. They had employed a party of villagers to beat the jungle, and all day I could hear their drums throbbing in the distance. This did not prevent me from finishing M.R. James or discovering a book called *A Naturalist on the Prowl* by Edward Hamilton Aitken.

My concentration was disturbed only once, when I looked up and saw a spotted deer crossing the open clearing in front of the bungalow. The deer disappeared among the sal trees, and I returned to my book.

Dusk had fallen when I heard the party returning from the hunt. The great men were talking loudly and seemed excited. Perhaps they had got their tiger. I put down my book and came out to meet them.

'Did you shoot the tiger?' I asked excitedly.

'No, my boy,' said Uncle Henry. 'I think we'll bag it tomorrow. But you should have been with us—we saw a spotted deer!'

There were three days left and I knew I would never get through the entire bookshelf. So I chose *David Copperfield*—my first encounter with Dickens—and settled down on the veranda armchair to make the acquaintance of Mr Micawber and his family, Aunt Betsy Trotwood, Mr Dick, Peggotty, and a host of other larger-than-life people. I think it would be true to say that *David Copperfield* set me off on the road to literature; I identified with young David and wanted to grow up to be a writer like him.

But on my second day with the book an event occurred which disturbed my reading for a little while.

I had noticed, on the previous day, that a number of stray dogs—belonging to watchmen, villagers and forest guards—

always hung about the house, waiting for scraps of food to be thrown away. It was ten o'clock in the morning, a time when wild animals seldom come into the open, when I heard a sudden yelp in the clearing. Looking up, I saw a large leopard making off into the jungle with one of the dogs held in its jaws. The leopard had either been driven towards the house by the beaters, or had watched the party leave the bungalow and decided to help itself to a meal.

There was no one else about at the time. Since the dog was obviously dead within seconds of being seized, and the leopard had disappeared, I saw no point in raising an alarm which would have interrupted my reading. So I returned to *David Copperfield.*

It was getting late when the shikaris returned. They were dirty, sweaty, and as usual, disappointed. Next day we were to return to the city, and none of the hunters had anything to show for a week in the jungle. Swear words punctuated their conversation.

'No game left in these... jungles,' said the leading member of the party, famed for once having shot two man-eating tigers and a basking crocodile in rapid succession.

'It's this beastly weather,' said Uncle Henry. 'No rain for months.'

'I saw a leopard this morning,' I said modestly.

But no one took me seriously. 'Did you really?' said the leading hunter, glancing at the book beside me. 'Young Master Copperfield says he saw a leopard!'

'Too imaginative for his age,' said Uncle Henry. 'Comes from reading too much, I suppose.'

'If you were to get out of the house and into the jungle,'

said the third member, 'you might really see a leopard! Don't know what young chaps are coming to these days.'

I went to bed early and left them to their tales of the 'good old days' when rhinos, cheetahs, and possibly even the legendary phoenix were still available for slaughter.

Next day the camp broke up and we went our different ways. I was still only half-way through *David Copperfield,* but I saw no reason why it should be left behind to gather dust for another thirty years, and so I took it home with me. I have it still, a reminder of how I failed as a shikari but launched myself on a literary career.

www.ingramcontent.com/pod-product-compliance
Lightning Source LLC
Chambersburg PA
CBHW020025030726
47499CB00007B/2270
9789355203441